THE VACATION

A Novel

SILK WHITE

Good 2 Go Publishing

THE VACATION
Written by Silk White
Cover design: Silk White
Typesetting: Mychea
ISBN: 9781943686698

Copyright ©2016 Good2Go Publishing
Published 2016 by Good2Go Publishing
7311 W. Glass Lane • Laveen, AZ 85339
www.good2gopublishing.com
https://twitter.com/good2gobooks
G2G@good2gopublishing.com
www.facebook.com/good2gopublishing
www.instagram.com/good2gopublishing

Printed in the USA

ACKNOWLEDGEMENTS

To all of you who are reading this, thank you for stepping inside the bookstore, stopping by the library, or downloading a copy of The Vacation. I hope you have enjoyed this read from top to bottom. My goal is to get better and better with each story. I want to thank everyone for all their love and support. It is definitely appreciated! Now without further ado Ladies and Gentleman, I give you *The Vacation*.

$ilk White

PROLOGUE

"**B**aby when you coming home?" Tasha whined into the phone.

"I'm on my way home now," Anthony Stone replied as he sat at a red light waiting for it to change. He was on a mission to get home at a decent time tonight. For the past two months, Anthony Stone had been hunting down a dangerous and violent man that went by the name, "The Genius". The Genius was said to be the mastermind behind several bank and armor truck robberies. The robberies were well planned and the capers got away every time leaving no clues behind. The robberies were so successful that the media named whoever the mastermind behind all the heist, The Genius.

"You promise?" Tasha asked, her tone filled with excitement.

"Yes, I'll be there in less than twenty minutes," Stone told her.

"Can you do me a big favor before you come home, please?"

"No favors tonight," Stone said playfully.

"Pleeeeease," Tasha sang doing her best baby voice impression.

Anthony Stone let out a loud sigh. "What do you want?"

"Can you get me some Chipotle please?"

"Damn I wish you would've said something sooner. I just passed it," Stone huffed as he made a quick U-turn. "I got you baby. I'll be there in a minute," he said ending the call.

Stone's black Dodge Charger pulled into the Chipotle parking lot where he killed the engine and stepped out of his vehicle and headed inside the restaurant. On his way towards the register Anthony Stone noticed two men sitting at a table talking loud while they enjoyed their meal. As Stone passed the two men, he noticed one of the men had blood on his shirt. Immediately his antennas went up. Stone stood on the line and discreetly observed the two men. They were two rough looking bad asses. The way they carried themselves screamed trouble. One guy wore his hair in cornrows while his partner sported a long blonde ponytail. A sleeve of tattoos covered both men arms.

Not being able to help himself Anthony Stone headed in the two men direction. He had no probable cause to arrest the two men so he planned on making small talk with them just to see where their heads were at. "Excuse me brother; do you have the time?" he asked politely.

"Fuck off cock sucker!" the man with the cornrows spat not even bothering to look up at Stone.

Anthony Stone stood there eyeing the two men. He badly wanted to reply but, from the looks of the two men, he knew if he did, things more than likely would go from bad to worst within a blink of an eye.

"Mother fucker!" The man with the ponytail stood to his feet with a dangerous look on his face. "You hard of hearing or something?!"

"I apologize," Stone threw his hands up in surrender and went back to his place in line. Just from the men's attitude, he could tell that the duo was up to no good.

"Can I help you, sir?" the server that stood behind the counter asked with a friendly smile. Anthony Stone looked over his shoulder and noticed the two tough guys making their exit. The voice in his head spoke loudly, *"Don't you go follow them! Order your food and go home to you woman who's waiting for you. Your woman that you promised you would spend time with. Don't do it!"*

"No thank you," Stone replied as he stepped out of line and followed the two guys out into the parking lot. He watched as the two men hopped in an Acura. Stone waited until the Acura pulled out of the parking lot before he raced to his Charger and followed the Acura making sure to stay at least three car lengths behind in distance so he wouldn't get detected.

Anthony Stone had no idea what the two men were up to but, from the way they carried themselves, it could only be trouble. He prayed he was wrong but, nine times out of ten when Stone followed his gut he was right. The Acura pulled in front of an old beat down house. Stone parked two blocks away and hit the lights as he watched the two men exit the Acura and make their way towards the trunk of the car. The two opened the trunk and pulled out what looked to be a dead body rolled up in a carpet. At first Stone wasn't sure if there was really a body rolled up in the carpet or not until he spotted the burgundy stain on the rug which looked to be blood from whoever the person was rolled up in the carpet.

"Shit!" Anthony Stone cursed as he called for backup and stepped out of his vehicle. He pulled his 9mm from the holster on his hip in a snapping motion and headed towards the rundown looking house. Protocol would be to wait for backup but, Anthony Stone didn't follow protocol. Instead he decided to take matters into his own hands and gamble on his instinct and judgment. Stone hopped the fence and jogged towards the front door. When he reached the door, he grabbed the doorknob and gave it a turn.

Locked.

Stone pulled a pocket knife from his pocket and jimmied his way inside the front door. The old door opened with a loud drawn out squeak. Anthony Stone pulled his Maglite from his back pocket and let the light guide him through the old house. Stone eased throughout the house with caution as the sound of a man yelling could be heard coming from somewhere inside the house.

"Bitch make another noise and I'll blow your fucking head off!" the voice screamed coming from a small door that Anthony Stone believed lead down to the basement. Stone snatched the door open and spotted a set of stairs that lead downstairs. He made an attempt to make his way down the stairs but, stopped short when he felt a sharp blade being pressed up under his neck from behind.

"Drop that fucking gun boy," the man holding Anthony Stone at knife point growled in a strong whisper.

"Before you do something stupid, I think you should know that I'm a cop," Anthony Stone said. "What do you say that you put that knife down and let's talk about this like men?"

The man pressed the knife even further into Anthony Stone's neck. "Drop that gun right now or I'm going to gut you like a fish!" It sounded more like a promise then a threat so Stone slowly dropped his gun to the floor and raised his hand in surrender.

"Now kick it over there!" The knife man nodded over towards the living room. Anthony Stone kicked the gun and spun in the same motion landing an elbow to the side of the knife man's head sending him stumbling backwards. The knife man regrouped and charged Anthony Stone. The knife man threw several knife strikes. Stone jumped back avoiding the knife by a centimeter. The knife man tried to jab the knife in Anthony Stone's chest and make good on his promise to gut the detective like a fish. Stone grabbed the knife man's wrist in mid swing and landed two strong blows to man's ribcage as the two men proceeded to tear up the entire living room. Anthony Stone slammed the knife man's arm into the wall forcing him to drop the knife. The knife man delivered a head butt to the bridge of Anthony Stone's nose, then scooped him up in the air and slammed him down through the vintage glass coffee table. Stone quickly bounced back to his feet and ducked a wild right hook and landed a three punch combo of his own. He went in for the knockout blow but, the knife man weaved the blow and countered with a side kick that landed in the center of Anthony Stone's chest sending him violently crashing through a wooden door. Anthony Stone hit the floor hard, rolled, grabbed his gun off the floor in the process, and aimed it at the knife man. "Get on your knees and place your hands on top of your head!" Anthony Stone commanded. The knife man ignored the command and continued on towards the detective. The knife man picked the knife up off the floor, let out an animalistic growl, and charged Anthony Stone.

Stone quickly dropped the knife man with four shots to his chest. Anthony Stone went to go check the pulse of the knife man when the door to the basement busted open and the two tough guys from the restaurant came through the door blasting.

Anthony Stone took off in a sprint as bullets peppered the wall following his every move. Stone fired two reckless shots over his shoulder before diving over the counter. He placed his back up against the counter and stuck a fresh clip into the base of his gun. The sound of the two tough guys moving throughout the living room could be heard. Stone got up on one knee when the sound of two different guns could be heard being fired. He stuck his arm around the counter and blindly fired off four shots. Seconds later, he heard the sound of the two tough guys running out the front door.

Stone slowly stood to his feet with a two handed grip on his weapon. He bent down and picked his Maglite up from off the floor. After making sure the living room was clear, Stone headed down to the basement. He turned the corner and saw three women tied down to three separate chairs. From the looks of things, the women had been beaten and violated. Anthony Stone walked over towards the women when he heard footsteps quickly approaching from behind. Stone spun around and spotted a man running towards him carrying a machete. Stone didn't hesitate to put a bullet in the man's head. The man awkwardly hit the floor. His foot shook for a few seconds, then it finally stopped indicating that the man was dead.

Anthony Stone untied the three women and led them upstairs where several other law enforcement officials were entering the home. Once the women were safe, Stone proceeded to look around. He headed back down to the basement to try and figure out exactly what had been going on down there. As he was looking around, he heard the sound of a cell phone ringing. Stone quickly searched the dead man's pockets and retrieved the phone. Flashing across the screen was the name, "The Genius". Anthony Stone cut the phone on and placed it up to his ear but, he didn't say anything.

"Who is this?" the voice on the other end asked.

"Detective Anthony Stone," he answered. "Is this The Genius?"

"No detective...I'm your worst nightmare," the voice on the other end growled before the line went dead.

Anthony Stone tried to call the number back but, it went straight to voicemail.

An FBI agent made his way down to the basement. "Hey you!" he said as he pointed at Anthony Stone. "Upstairs now!"

Stone made his way upstairs where a man in an expensive suit stood before him. "Who the hell are you?"

"Detective Anthony Stone," he replied.

"Well asshole, you just screwed up a two year investigation!" the expensive suit barked. "The Genius was on his way here tonight and we were finally going to nail that fucker tonight but, you screwed it all up!"

Anthony Stone's eyes drifted down to the floor. "I'm sorry I had no clue."

"Not as sorry as you're going to be! Now get the hell out of my sight!" expensive suit yelled dismissing the detective.

THE VACATION

CHAPTER 1

The next day when Anthony Stone stepped foot in Captain Fisher's office, he immediately could tell that he was about to get chewed out. "Captain, I can explain..."

"Save it!!!" Captain Fisher barked cutting Anthony Stone off. He was sick and tired of the detective's excuses. This was the detective's fourth write-up in the last eight months. "You messed up a two-year investigation," he paused to take a sip of his coffee. "We were this close to finally seeing what the Genius looks like," he said pinching his index finger and thumb together. "And now thanks to you, he's dropped off the radar."

"Captain, I saw two men pulling a dead body out of their trunk. What was I supposed to do?"

"Wait for back up!" Captain Fisher barked. "That's what you should have done!"

"I'm not that kind of cop," Anthony Stone said defiantly. He was an old school cop that most people would refer to as an action freak.

"You still drinking?" Captain Fisher asked with a raised brow.

"What does that have to do with anything?" Stone asked making sure not to answer the question.

"I see," Captain Fisher said giving the detective a sad look. "You're suspended for a month without pay!"

"Come on Captain!" Anthony Stone said shooting to his feet. "This is bullshit and you know it! I stopped something big from going down last night and saved lives in the process and you going to suspend me?!"

"The higher ups want you out of here," Captain Fisher told him. "I've protected you for as long as I can. It's out of my hands now."

Anthony Stone shook his head. His job was his entire life and here Captain Fisher was trying to take the only thing he loved away. "Captain, all I need is one last chance and I promise I won't fuck it up."

"It's out of my hands," Captain Fisher said quickly. "You have a month to get your shit together and if I were you, I would try to stop drinking because it's beginning to cloud your judgement."

"Captain, what am I supposed to do for a whole month?" Anthony Stone asked with a defeated look on his face.

"Are you still with that girl; what's her name...Tiffany?" Captain Fisher asked.

"Her name is Tasha and yes we're still together."

"Yeah Tasha, that's her name," Captain Fisher said suddenly remembering. "Why don't you take that nice girl of yours on a vacation?"

3

"The Genius is out here tearing shit up and you want me to take a vacation?" Anthony Stone couldn't believe his ears. "I signed up to do *real* police work not this bullshit!"

Captain Fisher stood to his feet. "You watch your tone in my office!" he yelled with a pointed finger. "You fucked up! Not me! Now you have to deal with the consequences!"

"Are we done here?"

"Get the hell out of my office!" Captain Fisher growled. He was afraid if the detective stayed a minute longer that a fist fight would break out between the two.

CHAPTER 2

Tasha stood in front of the stove making some Chicken Alfredo, sipping on some red wine while, Jill Scott's voice hummed softly in the background. She had just received a text from Stone notifying her that he was on his way home so she decided to make him a nice home cooked meal. Tasha hit a two step in the living room when she heard the front door open. "Hey baby," she sang in a happy voice as she danced her way over towards

Anthony Stone. Tasha grabbed Stone's waist with one hand swaying her hips to the beat. Instantly she could see that something was wrong. "What's the matter baby?"

Anthony Stone walked over to the kitchen and poured himself a vodka and orange juice then flopped down on the couch. "I got suspended today for a whole month."

"I'm sorry baby," Tasha said sitting down next to Stone while beginning to gently rub his back. "It's going to be okay." She knew just how much Anthony Stone's job meant to him so she could feel his pain. "What did they say?"

"Told me I should go on a vacation," Anthony Stone said taking a sip of his drink. He then chuckled. "All this for saving three lives and stopping something big from going down on my watch."

"It's going to be okay baby," Tasha kissed him on the cheek. "And maybe they're right."

"You think they're right for suspending me?"

"No I think a vacation would do you some good," Tasha smiled. "You don't really have a lot of time for me because of your job so we could go on a vacation and spend some quality time with one another."

Anthony Stone forced a smile on his face. "I guess you're right baby." Maybe a vacation was just what the two of them needed. Honestly Anthony Stone was surprised that Tasha hadn't left him yet with how busy his work kept him. It was new case after new case and still Tasha remained by Anthony Stone's side. "Set it all up and we'll go wherever you want to go."

Tasha hopped on top of Stone with excitement. "Are you serious? Anywhere I want to go?"

"Yes but, please take it easy. I'm not rich," Stone reminded her as Tasha planted wet kisses all over his face and neck. The more Tasha kissed him, the lower her kisses went until Anthony Stone's pants were around his ankles.

CHAPTER 3

The Genius stepped foot on the private plane with a neutral expression on his face. He wore an all-black Italian suit and anyone with a trained eye could tell that he was packing from the bulge that protruded near his hip. "Is everything ready to go?" he asked his second in command, a man that went by the name, Rambo. He got that name because he wore his hair in the same style as Sylvester Stallone in the movie, not to mention his love for guns. Unlike The

Genius, Rambo was dressed in combat gear. He wore all black, combat boots, black gloves, and a black bullet proof vest protected his chest.

"We all ready to go," Rambo said with a no nonsense look on his face. The plane was filled with forty-five soldiers and they were all dressed like Rambo. The two men sat down as the plane picked up speed and took off.

"Now tell me where is this boat headed?" The Genius asked as he placed his laptop on his lap and began clicking away on the keyboard.

"It's a cruise ship so it's going to make several different stops," Rambo explained. "We are going to gain access to the ship in Miami."

"How many passengers are projected to be on board?" The Genius asked never taking his eyes off of the screen on his laptop.

"Four thousand passengers," Rambo answered. "Each passenger is projected to have about two thousand dollars' cash on them to spend so that's about eight million in total. Not to mention, we have all the technology to gain access to all of their bank accounts from their bank cards, not to mention how much money the ship is going to be carrying," he pointed out.

"I'm projecting us to take in around fourteen million," The Genius spoke softly.

"What's our exit strategy?" Rambo asked. Knowing how the Genius operated, he knew the man liked to prepare for any and everything. His motto was, "Anything that could go wrong, would go wrong!"

"The first stop the ship is going to make will be in Jamaica," The Genius said. "That's where we will make our exit."

Once the plane was in the air, The Genius and Rambo unfastened their seatbelts and stood to their feet. "Show me where these two assholes are," The Genius said in a cool and calm tone. Rambo led The Genius towards the back of the plane and stopped in front of the two tough guys from Chipotle.

"These are the two that led the detective to the house," Rambo said standing over the two men.

"Boss I can explain," the man with the cornrows spat. "We were just doing our job and had no clue that we were being followed."

"I see," The Genius said in a calm tone. Without warning, he turned and slapped the taste out of the man with the cornrows mouth. He roughly snatched the man out of his seat and delivered a sharp knee to the man's stomach forcing him to double over in pain.

"I'm sorry," the man with the cornrows said in between coughs. "You know I would never cross you. I'd cross my own mother before I cross you," he pleaded. The Genius slowly walked over towards the small side door in the center of the plane and pulled down on the latch. A strong gush of wind immediately flooded the plane. The Genius pulled his .380 from the holster on his hip and shot the man with the cornrows in the chest five times killing him in cold blood in front of everyone on the plane. He watched as Rambo and another soldier grabbed the dead body and tossed it off the plane.

The Genius then headed over towards the second tough guy responsible for leading the cops to their location. "So what's your story?"

"We did everything you asked us to do," the man with the blonde ponytail said trying to sound strong but, The Genius could see the fear in the man's eyes. "It was no way to tell that the cops were tailing us, I swear."

A soldier standing next to The Genius handed him a metal baton. The Genius wasted no time using it. He swung the baton with so much force that it whistled through the air before making contact with the guy with the blonde ponytail's skull. The Genius continued to beat the man with the metal baton until the man finally stopped moving. Rambo and another soldier quickly grabbed the body off the floor and tossed it off the plane as if it was a bag of trash.

The Genius adjusted his suit jacket and took his seat. "How long until we get to Miami?"

CHAPTER 4

Anthony Stone and Tasha stood on line waiting to walk through the metal detector at the airport. They placed all of their belongings inside then took turns walking through the metal detector. Anthony Stone noticed the huge smile on Tasha's face as she put her shoes back on. This was the happiest he had saw her in a very long time. Due to his job and the long hours he worked, it made it hard for them to spend a lot of quality time together so this vacation was just what they're relationship needed. Stone held Tasha's hand as they walked through the terminal.

"I'm so excited," Tasha sang looking up at Stone.

"I've never been on a boat ride before," Anthony Stone shamefully admitted.

"You're going to love it," said Tasha. "Besides, I think it's going to be romantic."

"Of course you would say that," Anthony Stone said playfully.

"There are plenty of activities for us to do on the cruise," Tasha pointed out. She was just so excited to be spending some quality time with her man.

"I hope I don't have to arrest anyway on this cruise," he joked.

Tasha gave Anthony Stone a "don't play with me" look. "Repeat after me," she said looking him in his eyes. "While on vacation, I am not a cop and I will be on my best behavior and not think about work while on this trip."

Anthony Stone sighed as he repeated everything Tasha said word for word. His mind was still kind of on The Genius but, he quickly erased those negative thoughts from his head. His main focus for the next week was to make sure Tasha was happy and having a good time.

Anthony Stone boarded the plane and couldn't wait for the stewardess to come around so he could get himself a drink. Tasha sat next to Stone, looked him in the eyes, and kissed him on the lips.

"What was that for?"

"Just for being you," Tasha replied with a smile. "I know your job keeps you very busy but, I also know that you work extremely hard to keep the world safe from all these psychos out here in the streets."

"Thank you for always having my back baby," Anthony Stone said sincerely. It took a strong woman to love a man like him.

"During this vacation I don't want you to lift a finger," Tasha said in a seductive tone. "I'm going to wait on you hand and foot."

"Is that right?"

"Yes! I just want my king to enjoy this vacation. This is going to be the best vacation ever!"

***

Stone and Tasha sat in the backseat of the cab hand in hand. He was trying to enjoy his lady and this special time but, his mind was still on his suspension. He still couldn't believe that they suspended him after saving three lives and breaking up whatever plan The Genius had worked so hard on creating. The Genius was responsible for several big time heist that made the headline on every media outlet but, what bothered Anthony Stone the most was that no one had any clues on how to find The Genius. Even that wasn't what bothered Anthony Stone the most; what really bothered him was the fact that no one even had a clue what the man even looked like. The Genius was definitely one of the smartest criminals Anthony Stone had ever had the pleasure of hunting.

"What are you over there thinking about?" Tasha asked snapping Stone out of his thoughts.

"Sorry baby, I was just thinking about how much fun we are going to have on this vacation," Anthony Stone said placing a hand on Tasha's inner thigh.

"Hmmp!" she huffed. "Don't start nothing you can't finish."

The two shared a laugh and spoke about all the different things there was to do on the cruise. Anthony Stone sipped on his drink and listened to Tasha excitedly explain all of the activities that were available for them to partake in. Stone smiled and did his best not to think about The Genius or getting suspended. This time was supposed to be dedicated to him and Tasha.

***

"Isn't this nice?" Tasha asked with an excited look on her face as her, Stone and the rest of the guest all boarded the ship. The boat was huge and the employees on the ship were extremely nice. As Anthony Stone walked throughout the ship, he felt good about taking this vacation with Tasha. He had to put his personal feeling aside because this vacation wasn't about him, instead it was about Tasha and making her happy. "Aren't you excited?"

"Yes, this place looks great," Stone said as he passed several bars on the way to their room. He couldn't wait to relax and have several drinks. Anthony Stone rolled him and Tasha's luggage to their room and smiled when Tasha opened the door and they looked inside. The room was bigger than he expected. Stone walked inside taking note of the huge floor to ceiling mirrors. "I like this," he said noticing the king sized bed. The room even had a small kitchen area in it as well. The luxury room put Anthony Stone and Tasha's apartment to shame.

"I'm going to take a quick shower you. Wanna come join me?" Tasha said with a naughty smirk on her face.

"No baby, you go ahead. I'm going to walk around for a little bit so I can get a feel for everything that's on this ship."

"Okay well can you be back by the time I get out of the shower please?" Tasha asked.

"I'll see what I can do," Stone said slapping Tasha on the ass and exiting the room.

As soon as Anthony Stone stepped out of the room, he spotted two beautiful African American women walking pass his room.

"Hey handsome," the one with long pretty eyelashes said with a bright smile on her face.

Anthony Stone double checked to make sure his room door was closed before he answered. "Hey, how are you lovely ladies doing?"

"We're headed to the bar. Would you like to join us?" Eyelashes asked waiting for a response.

Anthony Stone thought about it for a second. He knew if Tasha found out he was hanging out with two beautiful women alone, it would look suspicious and more than likely cause problems in his relationship. "I don't know."

"Come on, one drink ain't going to hurt you," Eyelashes said grabbing a hold of Anthony Stone's hand and leading him towards the bar. "I'm Brittany and this is Monica."

"Nice to meet you both. I'm Anthony," he said with a smile. He could tell from how the two ladies kept looking at him that a drink wasn't all they wanted.

"So Anthony, you live out here?" Brittany raised her glass for a slow sip.

"No, I live in New York with my girlfriend," Anthony Stone slipped that in there to let the ladies know that he was taken.

"Wow! I always wanted to go to New York," Brittany said ignoring the part about him having a girlfriend. "Maybe when I come out there to visit you can show me around."

"Yeah, you could show the both of us around," Monica chimed in from the sideline.

Anthony Stone sipped his drink and looked over his shoulder to make sure Tasha wasn't trying to sneak up on him from behind. "So, do y'all go on cruises a lot?" Stone tried to change the subject.

"No but, if I knew handsome men like you were on cruises, I would have been taking cruises," Brittany said as she hungrily undressed Anthony

Stone with her eyes. Anthony Stone noticed Monica leave the bar with some muscular guy wearing a wife beater, leaving him and Brittany alone. Brittany grabbed Anthony Stone's hand and slowly caressed it. "You have some strong hands. What do you do for a living?"

"I'm a cop," he replied.

"A cop?" Brittany echoed with excitement. "How exciting!" Her hands slowly made their way onto Anthony Stone's back where she gently began to rub in circular motions. "Is that why you're in such good shape?"

Anthony Stone smiled. "I try to do my best."

"Well your best looks amazing," Brittany licked her lips. "So what are you doing later?"

Stone went to reply when, Tasha leaned over his shoulder seeming to appear out of the clear blue sky. "He'll be spending time with his girlfriend, sweetie." She looked Brittany up and down.

Brittany stood to her feet. "I was just making conversation. I'm not trying to step on anyone's toes," she smiled at Tasha then turned her gaze back on Anthony Stone. "I'll catch you later Mr. Stone," Brittany winked, spun on her heels and, then disappeared into the crowd.

"So, I take a shower for ten minutes and this is what you out here doing?" Tasha said with an attitude.

"Baby it wasn't even like that. I..."

"Well what's was it like then?" Tasha cut him off. "You brought me on vacation to embarrass me?"

Anthony Stone grabbed Tasha by the waist and pulled her in close. "Baby calm down...You know I would never disrespect my baby."

"Hmmp!" she huffed. "I can't tell," Tasha rolled her eyes.

Anthony Stone pulled Tasha down onto his lap and ordered her a drink. He knew him sitting alone talking to a beautiful woman looked suspect on his part. "They have a club downstairs," Stone smiled. "How about we go get our slow dance on?"

Tasha sipped her drink and smiled. "And don't think just because I dance with you that we're back friends."

***

Anthony Stone stood on the dance floor with his hands on Tasha's hips as her body swayed perfectly to the music. Anthony Stone looked around at all the people in the club enjoying themselves and having a great time when it finally dawned on him that he hadn't been enjoying his life. Stone had been so caught up in his job over the years that he now realized that he'd been depriving himself the opportunity to live and enjoy life. He looked around the club and saw that everyone was having a good time and enjoying themselves. *"This vacation is just what I needed,"* Stone thought to himself.

CHAPTER 5

"How much longer?" The Genius asked with a calm look on his face. He had been planning this heist for the last month and was excited to finally be about to pull it off. Being able to outsmart the authorities is what gave him a rush. The fact that he could steal millions of dollars and no one even had a clue as to what he even looked like made him feel invincible.

"Ten minutes," Rambo answered.

"We got all our weapons ready to go?"

Rambo nodded his head. "And I just spoke to a few of our men that's already on the ship and they're all in position."

"Good work," The Genius stood to his feet and grabbed his parachute and goggles. Rambo opened the back door to the plane and all the soldiers began strapping on their parachutes. Each soldier was armed to the tee and given simple instructions. The Genius stood on the sideline as he watched the first four soldiers dive off the plane. Then another four, then another four until it was only him and Rambo left on the plane. The Genius gave Rambo a hug. "I'll see you at the bottom," he said as they both ran and dived off the plane. The Genius' suit violently flapped in the wind as he floated through the air in what looked like a slow speed but, in all reality he was falling from the sky at a very high speed. The Genius flicked his wrist and checked the time on his watch. His soldiers should have landed on the ship by now.

***

The first four soldiers slowly landed onto the ship. They quickly removed their parachutes and tossed them over board into the water. Each man held an AR-15 assault rifle, wore all black, and covering their faces were gas mask.

"Hey, what hell is going on!?" a security guard who stood patrol asked when he saw four mask men approaching him. The first gunman violently jabbed the security guard in the face with the butt of his rifle breaking the guard's nose instantly. Without warning the next gunman close lined the security guard over the rail sending him over board. Seconds later, the sound of his body splashing loudly in the water could be heard. The next gunmen quickly ran up the steps and kicked the door open. Inside the room stood the captain of the ship and his crew. The gunmen opened fired and gunned down each man in cold blood. "Clear!" he yelled back to the other gunmen.

***

Over on the other side of the ship, a group of people stood around looking at the beautiful view of the water when a little kid tapped his mother, then pointed up to the sky. The boy's mother looked up and saw several men drop down onto the ship on parachutes. The four gunmen tossed their parachutes over board then wasted no time gunning down the group of passengers who stood around minding their business.

A security guard rounded the corner and spotted the four gunmen up ahead tossing passengers bodies off the side of the ship. *"Holy shit."* he said to himself as he pulled his .357 from his holster. The guard then quickly pulled his walkie-talkie from his waist and informed the rest of his security crew on what was going on. Having no time to waste, the guard knew he had to make a move and he had to make it now. The guard quickly sprung from behind the wall he stood behind and opened fire on the gunmen.

Bang! Bang! Bang!

One of the guard's bullets hit one of the gunmen in the neck dropping him instantly. The other gunmen quickly returned fire. Their bullets riddle and rocked the guard turning his body into Swiss cheese. The gunmen checked the pulse of their fallen comrade when they saw Rambo and The Genius land gently onto the ship. The Genius quickly removed the parachute from his back. Unlike the rest of the gunmen, he wore an expensive all-black suit and no mask covered his face.

The Genius turned to Rambo, "I'm going to blend in with the rest of the crowd. You know what to do." He hugged Rambo, patted him on the back, and then disappeared around the corner.

"Everyone was given their assignments on the plane! No more talking! It's show time!" Rambo said in an excited tone.

Rambo snatched open the door to the restaurant and sent several shots into the ceiling. "Now that I have everyone's attention, I need y'all to listen up!" he yelled. "Follow my instructions and you'll get to live to see another day!" "First things first! I need everyone to lay face down on the floor and place your hands behind your back!" While Rambo kept everyone at gun point, the rest of the soldiers zip tied all of the hostage's hands behind their back and removed anything that could be worth any value and tossed it into the huge garbage bags. One garbage bag was for jewelry, another for wallets, and the last garbage bag was for cash.

"Line them all up in the corner over there!" Rambo ordered. He then called ten soldiers over and gave them another assignment. "There's a club downstairs. I need y'all to go and get that area under control." Rambo then turned to another group of soldiers. "And I need y'all to go around the ship and start getting everyone out of their rooms. I want everyone packed into this restaurant."

"Are they all going to be able to fit in here?" one of the gunmen asked.

"Just do what the fuck I say!" Rambo yelled in the gunman's face.

CHAPTER 6

Anthony Stone sat on one of the couches in the club with a bottle of water in his hand. He was sweating bullets and needed a quick rest. If it was up to Tasha, the two would be dancing all night. Anthony Stone sipped his water and closed his eyes for a second. All of the alcohol he had consumed was finally starting to kick in and it had him feeling a little woozy. Even with him feeling woozy and all, this was one of the best nights of Anthony Stone's life. For the first time in his life, he felt free; free from stress, free from his job, free from chasing down criminals and, free from trying to save the world. Anthony Stone propped his legs up on the couch when he saw Tasha heading his way with a drink in her hand.

"I know you ain't going to sleep on me over here?" Tasha asked as she helped herself to a seat on Anthony Stone's lap.

"I just need a second to recharge," Stone said with his eyes closed. Not only was his head spinning but, now his stomach was bubbling and making funny noises.

"But, baby this is my song!" Tasha whined poking out her bottom lip.

"Get up for a second," Anthony Stone sat up and stood to his feet. "I'll be right back baby. I have to use the bathroom."

"Are you coming back for real?" Tasha asked with a raised brow.

"Yeah I'll be right back. I promise," said Stone. "Don't worry about me. You just make sure you have a good time," he said before disappearing through the crowd. Anthony Stone turned the corner right on time. If he'd turned the corner a second later, he would have saw six mask gunmen headed towards the club.

The lead gunman entered the club, raised his rifle, and fired several rounds into the ceiling. Immediately the DJ shut the music off and the club goers looked for a place to run but, there were gunmen blocking both exits.

"Everybody on the motherfucking floor now!" the lead gunman yelled. He watched as his team of gunmen zip tied everyone's hands behind their backs and remove their wallets and any kind of jewelry they had on them. "Now that I have everyone's attention, I want you all to stand in a single file line and I'm going to escort you all to the restaurant with the rest of the guest.

"Fuck you!" a brave white man yelled. He looked strong like he either played football or lifted weights on a regular basis. "I'm not going anywhere with you!   If you're going to kill me, then you better..."

The lead gunman filled the strong man's body with bullets before he could even finish his sentence. "Anyone else have something to say!" He waved his smoking hot rifle around. "That's what I thought! Now let's get to this restaurant!"

Tasha stood with her hands behind her back and a scared look on her face. At first she thought someone was playing a cruel trick on everyone in the club but, the more time that passed by, she realized that this was no trick but, instead the real thing. Tasha followed the rest of the club goers out of the club, up the stairs, and down two long hallways that led to the restaurant. When they entered the restaurant, Tasha noticed there was a room full of hostages with zip ties on their wrist and frightened looks on their faces. The gunmen roughly shoved all of the hostages down to the floor.

"If I hear a peek out of anyone of you, I'm going to shoot you in the face!" the lead gunman warned. Tasha quickly did as she was told not wanting to catch a bullet. She glanced around the restaurant looking for any sign of Anthony Stone. After looking over all the hostages for the third time, Tasha was positive that Stone was not in the restaurant. Tasha's body jumped when she heard a loud series of gunshots rang out. All she could do was hope and pray that Anthony was not on the receiving end of those gunshots.

CHAPTER 7

Rambo shot one of the ship's security guards in the face at point blank range. He strolled through the ship making sure there weren't any stray passengers roaming around. Rambo had ordered his second team of soldiers to go door to door and make sure no passengers were hiding in their rooms. Rambo was the muscle and The Genius was the brains. The two made a great combination. Rambo jogged down the steps to a small room down in the cut that said "Employees Only" on the door and kicked the door open. The door swung open and Rambo barged into the room. Inside fourteen security guards stood standing around listening to music and conversing.

"Hey asshole's!" Rambo yelled grabbing everyone's attention. Once he had the room's attention, Rambo squeezed down on the trigger and swayed his arms back and forth until every last security guard was no longer breathing. He then walked and pumped an extra two bullets in each one of the guards just to be on the safe side. Rambo turned to leave the room when he was tackled down to the floor from behind. The impact from the fall caused him to drop his weapon. The guard managed to get his arm under Rambo's throat and applied a deadly chokehold.

Rambo growled as he slowly stood to his feet. He shot his arm back landing a sharp elbow into the guard's rib cage, he then violently flipped the guard over his shoulder and removed the huge hunting knife from his holster and jammed it down into the side of the guard's neck. Then he gave the handle a deadly twist sending a spray of blood all over the place. Rambo cleaned the blade of his hunting knife off on the guard's shirt before placing it back in its holster. Rambo walked over a few feet, picked his rifle up off the floor, and then headed back towards the restaurant.

***

Tasha sat on the floor Indian style with her hands zip tied behind her back along with the rest of the passengers. The difference between Tasha and the rest of the passengers was she was looking around for an exit. Tasha knew the gunmen were heavily armed so if she did decide to make a break for it, she would have to be extremely cautious and extra careful. Sitting down next to Tasha was a Caucasian male with blue eyes, brown hair, and he looked to be wearing an expensive black suit. His brown hair looked like it had been ruffled that along with the five o'clock shadow he sported make him look like a rugged business man.

"Don't even think about it," the man in the expensive suit said as if he was reading Tasha's mind. "Those men will kill you and then sleep like a baby."

"Well what are we supposed to do, sit around and just wait to die?" she asked in a harsh whisper.

"Right now that's the only option we have," the man in the suit replied. "Just be patient and I'll try to come up with something."

"Well you better come up with something quick!" Tasha told the stranger in the suit. She was beginning to panic and lose hope. This time was supposed to be about her spending some quality time with her man but instead here Tasha was sitting on the floor in a restaurant with her hands tied behind her back and she didn't have a clue where her man was. *"Where the hell is he at?"* she thought to herself.

CHAPTER 8

Anthony Stone jogged down the hall and quickly entered his room and rushed to the bathroom. His stomach was bubbling and he could no longer take it. He sat on the toilet and handled his business. His head was spinning a little bit from all the liquor and heat in the club. After thinking long and hard about it, Anthony Stone was happy about taking this vacation but, he knew if he didn't hurry back to the club, Tasha would surely come looking for him. Anthony Stone stood and cleaned himself off when he heard several gunshots ring out followed by a few loud screams.

"What the hell?" Anthony Stone said as he stepped out the bathroom and heard the screams getting louder and louder. From the sounds of the screams, Stone could tell that whatever was going on, it was going on close by. Anthony Stone quickly ran over to his luggage and realized that he didn't bring his firearm. "Shit!" He stood to his feet with a worried look on his face as he heard the room door next to his get kicked in. A loud scream erupted followed by a single gunshot. Stone looked around his room for anything he could possibly turn into a weapon. His eyes landed on a pencil that sat on the dresser. Stone grabbed the pencil as the door to his room got kicked in. A masked gunman stood in the doorway with a rifle trained on Anthony Stone.

Immediately Stone threw his hands up in surrender. "Don't shoot."

"Turn around!" the gunman barked. His rifle followed Anthony Stone's every move.

Anthony Stone slowly turned around with his hands raised in the air.

"Drop the fucking pencil!" the gunman ordered. Having no other choice Anthony Stone did as he was told.

"What do you say we talk about this like men?" Anthony Stone said trying to buy himself some time to come up with a plan. Once the gun was close enough, Anthony Stone spun around and swiped the barrel of the rifle to the left while moving his head to the right as the rifle discharged. In the process a bullet grazed his cheek. Anthony Stone and the gunman struggled for possession of the rifle tearing up the entire room in the process as the rifle fired several holes in the ceiling. The two men went crashing through the bathroom door. Once Anthony Stone heard the rifle click empty, he released his grip on the gun and landed a quick upper cut to the gunman's chin, a blow that stunned the man who was trying to kill him. Stone followed up with an elbow to the face. He knew he had to get rid of the gunman before one of his friends came to join the party. The gunman grabbed Anthony Stone and violently tossed him into the wall, then landed a crushing body blow that caused Stone to double over in pain. The gunman kneed Stone in the face. Stone took the blow well. Once he got a chance to regroup, Stone took a fighting stance and threw a jab that snapped the gunman's head back. He went to fire his second blow when he saw the gunman reaching for something in his waist.

Stone ran and tackled the gunman down to the floor before he got a chance to remove whatever he was reaching for in his waistband. Anthony Stone placed his hand around the gunman's neck when he noticed the lamp laying on the floor next to him. He quickly picked up the lamp and let out an animalistic growl as he bashed the gunman's face in with the lamp repeatedly until the gunman stopped moving. Stone stood to his feet and wiped the blood from his nose as he took a second to try and figure out what the hell was going on. He walked over to the window and peeked out the blinds and saw several gunmen roughly escorting guest down the hall. Stone quickly walked over to the dead gunman and removed a 9mm from his waistband, then grabbed his cell phone and dialed Tasha's number. He listened as the phone rang out then finally went to voicemail.

More loud yelling snapped Anthony Stone out of his thoughts. He walked over to the door cracking it just enough for him to see through. Down the hall he saw a gunman double checking each room to make sure no passengers were left behind.

"Shit!" Stone cursed knowing he was going to have to make a move and make one fast. "Think! Think! Think!" Stone said to himself.

Stone quickly snatched the door open, stepped out into the hallway, and dropped the gunman with two shots to the chest before he realized what had hit him. Anthony Stone jogged down the hallway and dialed Captain Fisher's number. On the third ring Captain Fisher picked up. "What do you want Stone?" he asked in an irritated tone.

"I'm on a cruise ship and I think it's being high jacked," Anthony Stone said in a strong whisper as he continuously kept peeking over his shoulder.

"Stone, now is no time for games!" Captain Fisher snapped. "Take your suspension like a man."

"Fuck that suspension Captain! I'm on a ship with over four thousand passengers and there's an army of gunmen on this ship shooting these passengers down like animals!" Anthony Stone explained. "I think this may be a hostage situation. I already took out two of the gunmen."

"How many gunmen are on board?" Captain Fisher asked. Stone now had his full attention.

"I'm not sure but, I've taken out two and saw around ten more," Anthony Stone replied. "But, I'm guessing if there's four thousand people on this ship then it would have to be at least fifty to a hundred gunmen on board. That's if I had to guess."

"Where's the ship headed now?"

"We just left Miami so our next stop is going to be…." A gunman roughly tackled Stone down to the floor from behind causing him to drop his gun and cell phone.

"Hello?   Detective   Stone?   Are   you   there? Hello?" Captain Fisher yelled into the phone as he heard the sound of two men battling on the other end of the line. "Shit!"

CHAPTER 9

Anthony Stone scrambled back to his feet and hit the gunman with a lightning fast four punch combination to the chest and face forcing him back into the wall. He went to land another punch when the gunman dipped low and scooped Anthony Stone's legs from under him dumping him on his head. The gunman delivered two blows to Stone's head. Stone flipped the gunman over and wrapped his hands around the gunman's throat. The gunman pulled a knife from his leg holster and tried to jab it into Stone's side but, Stone manage to catch the man's arm in mid swing. Stone grunted loudly as he reversed the direction of the knife. The tip of the blade was now pointed at the gunman's neck. "Argh!" Stone growled as he jammed the knife down into the gunman's throat.

He stood to his feet as he watched the gunman gargle and choke on his own blood before he stopped moving. Anthony Stone bent down and removed the knife from the dead man's throat, slipped it in his back pocket, then picked his gun up off the floor and continued on throughout the boat. He moved throughout the ship and spotted another gunman with his back turned towards him. Stone thought about shooting the gunman in the back of the head but, he knew the blast from the gun would draw unnecessary attention so he slowly pulled the knife from his back pocket and crept up on the gunman from behind. Once the time was right, Stone sprang into action. With the swiftness of a cat, he clamped his hand over the gunman's mouth and jammed the knife down into his neck. The gunman went down quick and easy. Anthony Stone dragged the dead man's body out of plain sight and removed his AR-15 as well. He needed all the extra ammo he could find. Stone reached down in his pocket for his cell phone and cursed when he remembered he had dropped it during the fight he had with one of the gunmen. He badly needed to know how many gunmen were on the boat if he had even a small chance at surviving. Stone disappeared inside one of the rooms and locked the door. He quickly walked over to the refrigerator, grabbed a bottle of water, and turned it up like a savage. After the phone call to Captain Fisher, he could only hope and pray that help was on the way.

CHAPTER 10

"I need S.W.A.T. on that ship before these maniacs began to kill the hostages!" Captain Fisher ordered. "I'm not sure how many gunmen are on the ship but, let's assume there's a lot." He didn't know what the terrorist gunmen were up to but, if it involved four thousand hostages, he knew it had to be something terrible.

"Do we have any eyes on the ship?" the Lieutenant asked.

"Yes I have one of my guys on the ship," Captain Fisher said proudly.

"Your man will probably be dead in the next ten minutes so let's see how quick we can get S.W.A.T. in there," the Lieutenant said.

"My man is going to give those terrorists a run for their money," Captain Fisher said. "Let's just be patient. I'm sure he'll contact me again."

"Didn't you say the phone went dead while you were talking to your man?" the Lieutenant said giving Captain Fisher a side eye. "Then let's assume he's dead and wait for these terrorists to call and make their demands."

"My guy has military training and skills beyond this world. He's good at surviving and even better at killing," Captain Fisher said with confidence. Detective Stone's cowboy antics is what kept him in trouble but, other than that the detective had superb skills and was the most talented detective he'd come across in a long time.

"Well your guy needs to call in and do so quickly so we can have eyes on that ship!" the Lieutenant said as he began to put a rescue mission in motion.

Captain Fisher was pacing the floor and thinking of his next move when his office phone rang. "Track the call and put it on speaker!" he yelled. Once everything was set, he then answered the phone. "Detective Stone is that you?"

"No this is The Genius speaking," the voice on the other line spoke in a calm manner. "Who do I have the pleasure of speaking with?"

"This is Captain Fisher speaking."

"Captain Fisher, listen to me and make sure you listen carefully. I'm not a man that likes to repeat himself," said The Genius. "I have a ship with over four thousand hostages on it. Either you do as I say or I'll put a bullet in each one of these hostage's head and personally toss them over board myself!" he threatened. "Number one, if any law enforcement officials try to board this ship, I will begin to kill all the hostages. Number two, I need a helicopter and five million dollars waiting for me when the ship arrives in Jamaica and I'll be in touch!" The Genius hung up in Captain Fisher's ear.

"Shit!" Captain Fisher cursed. "I need eyes on that damn boat!"

"Well I'm not sitting around waiting for your guy to make contact. I'm sending S.W.A.T. on that ship," the Lieutenant stated plainly. "We'll see how much of a genius he is with a bullet in his head."

"Lieutenant, I don't think we should test this guy especially with so many hostages on board," Captain Fisher pointed out. "Let's play it safe and wait to see if detective Stone calls."

"Your detective is probably already dead!" the Lieutenant barked. "We need our men on board for Christ sakes. We don't even know what this guy looks like!"

Captain Fisher clicked a few keys on his laptop. "I've been trying to catch this asshole for over three years now," he said turning his computer towards the Lieutenant. The Lieutenant glanced at the laptop and saw a picture of two men shaking hands. In the picture he could see one of the men's face but, not the face of the second man.

"Who the hell are these guys?" the Lieutenant asked with his face crumbled up.

"The first guy goes by the name Rambo. He's The Genius's right hand man and also the muscle," Captain Fisher explained.

"And who's the second guy?"

"The second guy is our man," Captain Fisher smiled. "That's The Genius."

"What is this some kind of joke?!" the Lieutenant barked. "We can't even see his face!"

Captain Fisher zoomed in on the picture. "You see that?" he asked. In the photo, a tattoo of a spider was on the wrist of the mystery man. "We know The Genius has a spider tattooed on his wrist."

"Just great," the Lieutenant said in a sarcastic tone. "Now we have to search for a guy with a tattoo of a spider on his wrist." He looked Captain Fisher up and down. "I'm sending S.W.A.T. onto that ship and that's final!"

CHAPTER 11

The Genius hung up the phone and turned and faced, Rambo. "Time for stage two of our plan." He knew that the authorities would try and board the ship and rescue the hostages and The Genius was well prepared for all of the F.B.I.'s tricks.

The Genius peeked inside a room over in the corner and saw six men dressed in plain clothes sitting in front laptops. Each man had several stacks of credit and bank cards that they had stolen from all of the passengers and were transferring all the funds into an offshore account that only The Genius had access to. So far everything was going according to plan. "I say we have about three to four hours before our company arrives," The Genius said.

Rambo went to respond when he heard his walkie-talkie squeak, followed by a voice on the other end.

"Hey, I think we have a threat on the ship," the gunman said through the walkie-talkie. "I just found three of our men dead."

"Find whoever that guy is and kill him!" Rambo ordered.

"Something we should be worried about?" The Genius asked with a raised brow.

"Not at all. My men will smoke whoever this guy is out within the next thirty minutes," Rambo assured The Genius. "One of the security guards probably slipped through the cracks."

"Find him and kill him!" The Genius ordered.

"Will do," Rambo said as he placed the zip tie back around the Genius' wrist and led him back out into the restaurant along with the rest of the hostages. Rambo escorted The Genius to the middle of the restaurant and then roughly shoved him down to the floor.

***

"Hey are you okay?" Tasha asked when she saw one of the gunmen roughly shove the man in the black suit down to the floor.

"Yes I'm fine," the man in the suit said. "I must have been in the bathroom longer than they would have liked for me to be."

"Did they hurt you?" Tasha asked, her voice full of concern.

"Nothing I can't handle," the man in the suit said downplaying the situation. "But I did manage to get this," the man in the suit flashed a small razor blade in his hand. "I'm going to get us out of here!" he whispered.

"Are you crazy?! They'll kill us!" Tasha replied.

"If we stay here we're as good as dead anyway so what's the difference?" the man in the suit asked.

"Let's just wait for help," Tasha said with a nervous look on her face. "My boyfriend is somewhere on this ship," she told the man in the suit. "He's a cop."

"Isn't he tied up with the rest of us?" the man in the suit asked.

"No. I don't think they caught him yet and, if I know my boyfriend the way I think I do, this is going to be a long night on this ship."

"I don't think I caught your name," the man in the suit said.

"Tasha," she answered.

"Brett," the man in the suit countered. "Nice to meet you. I just wish it were under better circumstances."

"Yeah me too."

"So, do you think your boyfriend is going to save us?" Brett asked.

"Yes," Tasha answered with confidence.

CHAPTER 12

Anthony Stone eased his way down a long hallway. He had heard loud screams nearby and was heading to investigate. He held a strong two handed grip on the A.R. 15 and continued along the hallway. Stone had no clue as to what was going on or what to expect. He was just simply trying to save as many lives as he could. When Stone reached the end of the hallway, he slowly peeked his head around the corner and saw two armed gunmen holding Brittany, the woman from the bar at gunpoint.

***

"Please don't hurt me. I have a family," Brittany pleaded with her hands up in surrender. "Why are y'all doing this?"

"Bitch shut the fuck up!" one of the gunmen barked as he turned and slapped Brittany down to the floor. The two gunmen grabbed Brittany and tried to zip tie her hands behind her back and drag her back towards the restaurant along with the rest of the hostages.

"Noooo!" Brittany kicked and screamed, refusing to cooperate. She knew if she allowed the gunmen to take her to that restaurant, it was a good chance that she wouldn't make it out of there alive. "No stop!...Stop!...Let go of me!"

Brittany looked up and watched as both of the gunmen's heads exploded spraying her face and the walls with blood. Brittany looked up and saw

Anthony Stone turn the corner holding a smoking gun in his hands.

"You okay?" Stone asked.

Brittany jumped up to her feet, ran and gave Stone a tight hug. "Oh my God! Thank you so much! You saved my life!"

"Who are these men and what do they want?" Stone asked.

"I don't know. All I know is, they have shot and killed over a hundred passengers," Brittany said in a frantic tone. "Are we going to die?"

"No. I'm going to protect you but, first I'm going to need your help." Anthony Stone leaned down so he could be closer to Brittany's ears so he could whisper. "Do you have any idea how many gunmen are on board?"

"I'm not sure but, if I had to guess, I would say about fifty to sixty gunmen," Brittany answered in a hushed tone.

"Where are they keeping all of the hostages?"

"They have them all in the restaurant," Brittany answered.

"Do you know how to get to the restaurant?" Anthony Stone asked.

Brittany nodded her head. "I don't think it'll be wise for us to go to the restaurant." Brittany had saw up close and in person how violent and dangerous the gunman were. "I think we should find somewhere for us to hide until all this blows over."

"I have to save all of those hostages," Stone replied. "My girlfriend is in that restaurant," he said as he fished through the dead gunman's wallet. The first thing he noticed was there was no ID in the wallet, nothing that could identify the gunman. "You know how to shoot?"

Brittany raised her hand and wiggled it from side to side. "Kind of," was her only answer. "I've been to the shooting range once or twice...why?"

Anthony Stone handed Brittany the 9mm from his waistband. "Here, you may have to use this."

Brittany grabbed the gun and studied it carefully for a few seconds. "I'm definitely going to have to use it, aren't I?"

Stone nodded his head. "More than likely...yes." All Brittany wanted to do was party and get laid and now she was being asked to take a human beings life if need be. Everyone on the ship was being put in a situation where it was either kill or be killed. "Brittany, I need you to promise me that if you get a shot on one of these gunmen that you're going to take it."

"I promise," Brittany said with a scared look on her face.

Anthony Stone and Brittany eased down the glass hallway that led to a small staircase when, Stone saw movement from the corner of his eyes. "Get down!" he yelled as he shoved Brittany down to the floor as bullets shattered the glass hallway and left big holes in the wall. Stone returned fire as he ran down the hall and dived in the staircase as several bullets peppered the wall where his head was two seconds earlier. Anthony Stone peeked around the corner and saw Brittany ducking down firing shot after shot blindly over her shoulder. The first gunman rounded the corner and Stone wasted no time putting him down with a bullet to the throat. After he gunned the first gunman down, the rest of the gunmen decided to play a game of cat and mouse. Stone tried to get Brittany's attention so she could let him know if she had eyes on any of the gunmen.

Once all the gunfire ended, Brittany shot to her feet and took off running in the opposite direction. As soon as she jolted from her hiding spot, the gunfire immediately started back up. A bullet grazed the side of Brittany's face dropping her in her tracks. The gunman reloaded his rifle as he took hurried steps towards the wounded woman. The gunman stood over Brittany with the business end of his rifle trained on her. Brittany shut her eyes and waited for the blast to come. Just as the gunman got ready to pull the trigger, Anthony Stone tackled him down to the floor. The gunman dropped his rifle and he fell a few feet away from Brittany. She quickly rolled over and picked the rifle up from off the floor.

Stone wrestled on the floor with the gunman. Each man fighting to gain the better position. Brittany stood to her feet and tried to aim the rifle at the gunman but, she couldn't get a good shot. Anthony Stone and the gunman stumbled to their feet and Stone threw a quick jab followed by an uppercut that stunned the gunman. Stone then finished the gunman off with a side kick that bounced off the gunman's head knocking him unconscious. Stone spun around and saw another gunman snatch the rifle out of Brittany's hand and toss her down to the floor. Before the gunman could shoot Brittany, Anthony Stone grabbed the rifle turning it up to the ceiling as the rifle discharged repeatedly causing both Stone and the gunman's ears to ring. Stone rushed the gunman against the wall. Once the rifle was empty, the gunman kneed Stone in the chest and then fired off a lightning fast five punch combination. Stone blocked all five punches and countered with two of his own. The gunman took the punches well, grabbed Stone and flung him into the wall. Stone hit the wall and slipped a knife from his waistband. When the gunman came in to follow up, Anthony Stone had already cut him four times before he even realized what was going on. The gunman threw a punch when Stone jammed the tip of the blade in the gunman's arm, then dragged the knife down to the palm of his hand, slipped behind him, and slit the gunman's throat.

Brittany looked up from the floor as the gunman's lifeless body crumbled down to the floor. The look on her face was a terrified one.

Anthony Stone extended his hand and helped Brittany to her feet. "You okay?"

Brittany nodded her head as she looked around at all the carnage. She couldn't believe how close she was to losing her life. "Who the hell are these men?"

"Your guess is just as good as mines," Anthony Stone replied as he searched the dead gunmen for weapons and ammunition. "None of these guys are carrying an ID."

"What the hell do they want?" Brittany asked.

"I don't know but, we have to keep moving." Stone grabbed Brittany's wrist and pulled her along.

"Wait I need a gun!" Brittany said.

"All I have is this one gun," Stone said sticking the 9mm in his waist. "And I only has four bullets left."

"So what the hell are we supposed to do?" Brittany asked with her voice full of panic.

"Here," he handed her the same knife that he had just killed the last gunman with. "It's all I got. I'll do my best to protect you," Stone said, then led the way down the hallway when he felt something sharp penetrate his side, seconds later the pain followed. "Argh!" Stone growled as he spun around and saw Brittany standing there with a bloody knife in her hand.

"Brittany what the hell are you doing?!" he asked with a confused look on his face. Brittany didn't respond, instead she charged Anthony Stone with the knife in her hand. The look on her face was no longer a scared one but, now a demonic one.

CHAPTER 13

B rittany swung the knife like a professional going straight for Anthony Stone's neck. Stone blocked the knife strike but, in the process received a nasty gash on his arm. Brittany professionally flipped the knife into her other hand not missing a beat as she attempted to stab Stone in his chest. He caught Brittany's arm in mid swing and swung her into the wall as he held a firm grip on her wrist that she held the knife with. In a quick motion, Brittany released her grip on the knife and caught it with her free hand before it hit the floor and sliced Anthony Stone across his face. Brittany followed up with another knife strike but, Stone blocked the attempt and bent Brittany's wrist back forcing her to drop the knife. He then landed a stiff elbow to Brittany's face sending her shuffling back a few steps. Stone was raised to never hit a woman but, in this case he had to put all that to the side and handle his business. He took a fighting stance as Brittany charged him. He side stepped Brittany's attack and landed a quick check hook that landed flush on Brittany's jaw. She fired back with a four punch combo that Stone blocked with ease and swept Brittany's legs from under her. Brittany jumped back to her feet with a smirk on her face. She faked low and came high with a kick to the head. Stone ducked the kick just in time as he watched Brittany's foot shatter the glass wall where his head once was. Anthony Stone did a front roll on the ground, picking up the knife in the process. With a quick flick of the wrist, he tossed the knife and watched as it flipped through the air before landing in Brittany's chest.

Brittany stood with a shocked look on her face as a dark red color began to fill her shirt. "Help me," she whispered. Anthony Stone walked up to Brittany, planted his feet, then side kicked the handle of the knife further into Brittany's chest until it was no longer visible.

Stone looked on as he watched Brittany lay on the floor taking her last breath. Once she was dead, Anthony Stone fished through her pockets looking for anything that could let him know who these people were and why they wanted to take over a cruise ship. During his search, Stone found a cell phone in Brittany's pocket. In her wallet, there was no identification just like the other gunmen. Suddenly, Anthony Stone heard loud footsteps coming down the hall. He quickly reached his hand in Brittany's open wound in her chest and pulled his bloody knife out knowing he would probably need to use it again in the near future. Once Stone retrieved his knife, he took off running down the hall and looked for a place to hide.

CHAPTER 14

Captain Fisher pulled up to the port where several small speedboats sat waiting to be driven out into sea to save all of the hostages from the high jacked ship. He knew this was a bad idea but, the higher ups thought it was better to be proactive instead of reactive. Captain Fisher watched as the S.W.A.T. members boarded the speed boats with all of their fancy equipment. *"This is a bad idea,"* he said to himself as the Lieutenant walked up to him with a smirk on his face.

"Time to put the women and kids to bed," the Lieutenant said. "The men are about to go hunting."

"So what's the plan?"

"We're going to send out twelve boats," the Lieutenant began. "The boats will be filled with four snipers on each boat." He paused for a second. "While those idiots on the ship will be focusing on the boat, we're going to have a helicopter in the sky that will drop down four of our best agents into the water and from there, they will swim under water until they reach the ship. When they reach the ship, they will board the ship, and take out each of them gunmen one by one."

"If you do that, there's a chance a lot of the hostages may be put at risk," Captain Fisher pointed out. "We don't want any of the hostages to lose their lives if they don't have to."

"If thirty to forty hostages have to lose their lives in order to save thousands, then so be it," the Lieutenant said showing no remorse. "We'll save thousands of hostages and eliminate The Genius all at the same time. Sounds like a win, win to me."

"I don't think we should rush into this Lieutenant!" Captain Fisher explained as he felt his cell phone vibrating on his hip. "Captain Fisher," he answered.

"Hey captain it's me."

"Stone?" Captain Fisher said in a light whisper walking off to the side so he could talk in private. "What the hell is going on?!"

"I've been stabbed and I'm bleeding badly," Anthony Stone said. "I took out several gunmen but, I think there's a lot more on board."

"Is The Genius on board that ship?" Captain Fisher asked.

"How the hell would I know? I don't even know what he looks like," Anthony Stone reminded him.

"He has a tattoo of a spider on his wrist."

"Huh?"

"The Genius has a tattoo of a spider on his wrist," Captain Fisher repeated.

"You think The Genius is behind this?"

"I know he is," Captain Fisher answered quickly. "The Lieutenant is about to send S.W.A.T. on board."

"He can't do that!" Stone snapped. "If they catch wind that S.W.A.T. is on board they'll began to kill the hostages and right now my girl, Tasha is one of those hostages so that can't happen!"

"It's out of my hands the Lieutenant has now officially taken over," Captain Fisher explained. "The best advice I can give you is, you better find and rescue those hostages before S.W.A.T. boards that ship."

CHAPTER 15

Rambo walked down the hall with a firm grip on his A.R. 15. So far in passing he had stepped over three dead bodies, bodies of men he'd personally trained himself, bodies of men he'd eaten dinner with. The site made Rambo sick to his stomach and what really bothered him the most was the fact that he had no idea who was responsible for all this chaos and the death of his men. Rambo strolled down the hallway and stopped when he found Brittany's body lying dead in the middle of the floor. From all the glass that surrounded the floor and all the bullet holes in the wall, Rambo could tell that an intense battle had taken place. He silently signaled for two of his men to go search around the corner. Rambo kneeled down and closed Brittany's eyes as he looked around and saw several more dead soldiers laying around. Just as Rambo was about to get upset, he spotted a trail of blood. He reached down and touched the blood. The blood was still warm which meant that the blood was fresh and more importantly whoever the blood belonged to was close by. "Ay boys!" he yelled. "Our target is wounded and close by," Rambo announced as him and his men got focused and followed the blood trail.

***

Anthony Stone moved down the hallway as fast as he could. The whole time he made sure to keep pressure on his side where Brittany had stabbed him. He cursed himself over and over again for letting his guard down and leaving himself open for the attack. Anthony Stone wasn't able to see how bad his wound was but, the pain was so bad that it forced him to walk with a slight limp. Not being able to take the pain any longer, Stone used his shoulder as a battering ram and busted his way into one of the rooms in his path. He took hurried steps to the bathroom where he searched high and low until he found a first aid kit. Stone winced in pain as he laid his gun on the sink and lifted his shirt up so he could get a better look at his wound.

Anthony Stone cursed as he stuck his finger in his wound to see how deep it was. "Arrrgh!" He quickly grabbed a bottle of rubbing alcohol and poured it all over his wound. Immediately his eyes snapped shut as the pain took over his entire body. Stone stuffed his wounds with cotton balls, grabbed a roll of duct tape, and wrapped the tape tightly around his waist in hopes that the pressure would help stop the bleeding.

A loud noise snapped Anthony Stone out of his train of thought quickly bringing him back to reality.

He grabbed his gun off the sink and headed straight to the window and peeked out. "Shit!" he cursed when he noticed two gunmen coming down the hallway headed in his direction. Not having much time, Anthony Stone knew he had to think fast. Stone snatched the door open, fired off four shots dropping the two gunmen before they got a chance to let off any return fire. Stone quickly ran over to the dead gunmen and removed one of the gunmen's machine gun and placed a handgun down in his waistband. As Anthony Stone went to walk off, one of the gunmen grabbed his ankle in a firm grip. Stone quickly spun around and shot the gunman's face off in cold blood. In a split second three more gunmen rounded the corner and opened fire on Stone.

Anthony Stone took off in a sprint down the hall as bullets pinged loudly off the walls and doors. Stone disappeared inside the staircase as several bullets decorated the staircase door. Stone turned the corner, tripped, and fell face first down a whole flight of stairs. It was a rough and bumpy ride that finally came to an end leaving Stone upside down with a gash on his forehead.

***

Rambo rounded the corner and opened fire on the target fleeing down the hallway running for his life. Rambo watched as the target dashed through the staircase door dodging a headshot by less than an inch. *"I know I hit that cocksucker!"* he said to himself as he jogged down the hall towards the staircase. Rambo placed his back up against the wall, then on a silent count of three, he ordered one of his comrades to snatch open the staircase. Once the staircase door was open, Rambo was the first one in the staircase with his finger wrapped around the trigger ready to fire. "Shit!" Rambo cursed when he saw that the staircase was empty. "He's wounded!" Rambo announced. "He won't make it far, so keep your eyes open and stay on point. We're going to flush this cocksucker out of the hole he crawled in!"

CHAPTER 16

Tasha sat on the floor Indian style with her hands tied behind her back with an aggravated look on her face. It had been hours since all the hostages had been tied down and not allowed to move, nor eat anything. Tasha felt like a caged animal sitting amongst all the strangers. "Hey!" she yelled out to one of the gunmen. "Hey you!"

"What!" the gunman growled in a foul tone as if he was the one that had been tied up and tossed in a room with a bunch of strangers for hours.

"I'm thirsty. Can I please have something to drink?" Tasha asked.

The gunman stared at Tasha for a few seconds and didn't say a word. Then he cleared his throat and spat in her face. "Drink that!" the gunman said disrespectfully then walked off.

"Asshole!" Tasha yelled as her eyes filled up and tears freely ran down her face. The fact that the gunman had spit in her face didn't bother her. What really bothered Tasha was the fact that her hands were tied behind her back not allowing her the opportunity to wipe the spit from her face, so for the moment she just had to sit there with spit on her face looking foolish.

"Hey!" Brett nudged Tasha with his foot to get her attention. "Hey!" he called out until finally, Tasha looked in his direction. Brett flashed his hands showing Tasha that he was free. Brett scooted over towards Tasha. "Hey, I'm going to cut you free and on the count of ten we are going to run to that door over there," he nodded towards the door he was talking about.

"Are you crazy? They'll shoot us down like we're animals!" Tasha said in a harsh whisper. "If we going to do this, then we need to come up with a solid plan."

"We don't have no time for that," Brett said while cutting Tasha's hands free. "We have to get out of here, plus didn't you say your husband was still somewhere on the ship?"

"Yes my boyfriend. He's not here with the rest of us. I just hope he's not..."

"Positive thoughts," Brett cut Tasha off. "Okay here we go...one...two..."

"Wait. Hold up. They're going to kill us," Tasha pleaded with a scared look in her eyes.

"Five...six....seven," Brett continued to count as he gripped Tasha's hand tightly. "Eight....nine....."

Tasha kicked her heels off and got ready to run, when a loud sound of gunfire echoed loudly from another section of the ship. Immediately most of the gunmen scrambled towards the direction where the gunshots were being fired.

"Come on!" Brett pulled, Tasha up to her feet and the two quickly took off in a sprint through the door.

"Hey!" one of the gunmen yelled as he opened fire on the couple trying to escape. Tasha and Brett slipped through the door just as bullets peppered the door.

"Come on!" Brett yelled as he pulled Tasha along as the two ran blindly throughout the ship dodging bullets. As Brett and Tasha rounded the corner, they ran dead into one of the gunmen. Without warning, Brett hit the guard with a rabbit punch that stunned the gunman. Brett then immediately grabbed the gunman's rifle with two hands. Tasha took cover behind a wall as she watched Brett and the gunman fight for possession of the rifle. A vicious battle that neither man wanted to lose, especially because whoever the loser of the battle was would more than likely lose his life next.

Brett head butted the gunman shattering his nose in the process, he then followed up with a knee to the gunman's groin forcing him to release his grip on the rifle. Brett quickly turned the rifle on the gunman and shot him in the face at point blank range.

Tasha covered her mouth with both hands as she watched the gunman's lifeless body crumble down to the floor. Brett sat the rifle down on the floor, then grabbed the gunman's body. "I need your help! Come grab his legs!"

Tasha tip toed over towards Brett and grabbed the dead gunman's legs. Brett and Tasha struggled to get the dead body in the air where they finally tossed his body over board. Brett grabbed the rifle with one hand and Tasha's wrist with the other. "Come on! We have to get out of here!"

As the two ran, they noticed two more gunmen up ahead making small talk. Brett quickly pulled Tasha inside one of the vacant rooms and shut the door behind them. "I'm going to need you to be extremely quiet!" he said in a harsh whisper as he noticed when he closed the door, the sound had grabbed the two gunmen's attention. Brett peeked through the blinds and saw the gunmen began to search each room on the line one by one all over again. The gunmen were only three rooms down forcing Brett to come up with a plan quick.

"Get under the bed!"

"Huh?"

"Get under the bed now!" Brett spat giving Tasha a little push. Once Tasha was under the bed, Brett went and hid behind a wall with his rifle aimed at the door ready to fire at will.

Tasha laid under the bed when her body jumped from the sound of the door being kicked open. She shut her eyes as she heard the loud sound of combat boots making their way inside. Tasha held her breath doing her best not to make a sound as the sound of the footsteps got louder and louder.

Brett stood holding a firm grip on the rifle. He couldn't see the gunmen but, he could feel that they were only a few inches away from rounding the corner.

Suddenly a noise erupted from outside the room. The noise grabbed the gunmen's attention, leading them outside to investigate what caused the noise.

Brett waited five minutes before he came out of his hiding spot, went and peeked out the window. "Okay, you can come from under the bed!" he called to Tasha. She slowly crept from under the bed.

"You don't think it would be a good idea for us to just stay in here and hide?" she asked in a light whisper.

"Now that they know we're gone, they'll be sure to come looking for us," Brett stated plainly. "We can stay here for a while but, then we'll have to find another spot to hide later."

Tasha was about to respond when the sound of loud gunfire sounded off loudly coming from somewhere on the ship. The gunfire paused for a second then picked up again.

"Damn!" Brett said. He knew for a fact that he could hear at least five different guns being fired all at the same time. He looked over towards Tasha and noticed a sad look on her face. "What's wrong?"

"I know those gunshots have something to do with my boyfriend," Tasha said as her eyes got watery as she spoke. "I just hope he's okay."

"I'm sure he's fine," Brett said trying to keep Tasha in good spirits. He definitely didn't need her breaking down at a time like this. "We have to focus on keeping ourselves alive right now."

Tasha nodded but, deep down inside there was no way that she could not worry about Stone. He was the love of her life and the man she planned on spending the rest of her life with.

Brett walked over to the refrigerator and pulled out two sandwiches that some couple must have prepared before they were captured. "Here you need to eat something," Brett said handing Tasha a sandwich along with a bottle of water.

Tasha took the bottle of water and took it straight to the head, guzzling it like a savage. She didn't realize how thirsty she was until she tasted the water. "I need a weapon," she said biting down into her sandwich.

"I'll work on it," Brett replied staying close to the window so he could peek out every few seconds. "Do you know how to shoot?"

"I'm a fast learner," was her answer. Tasha had never even touched a gun in her life but, she knew with the situation that she and Brett were put in, that would soon change. Tasha had already participated in tossing a dead body over board so she figured it couldn't be too much worse than that. "You ever been shot before?" she asked.

Brett shook his head. "No, and I plan to keep it that way." Brett knew Tasha was scared so he had to try and figure out a way to keep her calm so their chances of surviving would be better. "So tell me a little bit about your boyfriend."

"Well, he's a cop and his name is Anthony..."

"You mean to tell me that Detective Anthony Stone is your boyfriend?" Brett asked with his voice full of excitement.

Tasha nodded. "Yup that's my boyfriend."

"That guy is a hero!" Brett said. "I see him on the news all the time!"

"Yeah, he's kind of a local celebrity," Tasha admitted. "It's kind of a gift and a curse."

"I don't follow," Brett said with a confused look on his face.

"Sometimes our relationship has to be put on hold because of his job," Tasha said with a sad look on her face. "It's like everywhere we go, someone can always use his assistance," she chuckled. "He finally took time off from work so we could go on vacation and now this happens." At this very moment, all Tasha could do was laugh to try to keep from crying. Brett placed a comforting hand on Tasha's back.

"Your boyfriend's job is to try to help save lives," Brett said. "I know it's a tough job but, someone has to do it."

"At night time, it's really hard for me to sleep because I'm always hoping and praying that one of these maniacs out here don't kill him," Tasha volunteered. "Even right now, every time I hear gunshots I get nervous because I have no idea if he's dead or alive...I just have to hope and pray for the best."

CHAPTER 17

Anthony Stone eased out of the staircase and found himself inside a kitchen to one of the restaurants on the ship. Not sure if this was the restaurant with all of the hostages, Stone walked from the kitchen to the sitting area with extreme caution. His side was killing him but, he knew the show must go on. Stone exited the restaurant, strolled down the hall, made a right, and ended up outside on the ship. Up ahead Stone spotted a gunman standing guard at a post with his back turned to him. Stone quietly crept up on the gunman from behind and jammed a knife down in the side of his neck, taking him down to the floor in the process. Stone dragged the gunman's body out of plain sight and continued his search throughout the ship. Being as though the ship was so big it made it hard for Anthony Stone to search it from top to bottom as fast as he would have liked. He made it halfway down the hall when he heard movement from up above. Stone slowly looked up just as a body dove from off the second level, landing on his back.

A dark skin woman with wild hair landed on Stone's back, she immediately clamped her legs around his waist, and slipped a knife from the small of her back all in the same motion. Stone's survival instincts kicked in as his hand shot up, grabbing the wild hair woman's wrist, blocking the knife strike attempt. With her free arm, the wild hair woman wrapped it around Stone's throat and tried to choke him out. Without warning, Stone came forward, bending over, flipping the wild hair woman over his shoulder. A booming sound echoed loudly as her body violently bounced off the floor. In the process of her hitting the floor, the wild haired woman lost possession of the knife. Stone quickly hopped to his feet and grabbed the woman by her wild hair and landed four hard upper cuts to the woman's face turning it instantly from pretty to a bloody mess. He then grabbed the woman, lifted her up over his head, and tossed her overboard.

"Bitch!" Anthony Stone mumbled under his breath as he took a second to get himself together. The wild hair woman had definitely caught him off guard. He was just happy that their little scuffle didn't draw the attention of any of the other gunmen that were patrolling the ship. Stone dipped inside one of the millions of doors on the ship. This particular door led him to the area where the comedy shows were held. Anthony Stone quickly entered one of the aisles over in the corner and laid down. His body badly needed to rest. It had taken quite a beating, not to mention all of the alcohol he'd consumed earlier at the club. He made sure he was out of plain sight just

in case trouble came looking for him. The only good thing he had going for him was that the wound on his side had finally stopped bleeding. Now all he needed were a few pain pills and he'd be in heaven right now. Stone shut his eyes and his mind automatically went to Tasha. He hoped and prayed that she was okay and not somewhere in pain or scared to death. *"Don't worry baby I'm coming to get you."* he said to himself as he reloaded the A.R. 15. Stone pulled out the cell phone that he'd taken from one of the dead gunmen and dialed Captain Fisher's number.

"Stone!" Captain Fisher answered on the first ring. "You better be calling with some good fucking news!"

"Four more gunmen dead," Anthony Stone replied. "And a lot more to come before this is over with."

"Well you have about two more hours until the sun goes down," Captain Fisher explained. "Once the sun goes down, that's when the S.W.A.T. team is going to make their move." He paused for a second. "They're coming in firing at will just so you know."

"But there's thousands of hostages on board," Anthony Stone reminded the Captain.

"You know how S.W.A.T. plays. They'll sacrifice hundreds of hostages in order to save thousands," Captain Fisher stated plainly. "If you don't want that to happen, then you have two hours to save those hostages."

"I'll do my best," Stone said ending the call. He made it back to his feet and walked down the steps towards another door but, before he made his exit, he noticed a map of the entire ship plastered on the wall. He examined the map carefully until he finally located the restaurant. *"Don't worry baby; here I come."*

CHAPTER 18

After searching high and low for the brave Samaritan on the loose, Rambo made his way back to the restaurant in a foul mood.

"What's wrong?" another gunman asked.

"We have a good Samaritan with a happy trigger finger on the loose," Rambo replied as he walked over to the wall where he spotted what looked like a phone hanging off the wall. Rambo grabbed the receiver, put it to his ear, and pressed a few buttons on the base.

"Testing…testing…one…two…three…" His voice was now being broadcasted over the loudspeaker so everyone on the entire ship could hear him. "This message is for the tough guy running around with the machine gun playing hide and seek," Rambo began. "You got five minutes to make your way down to the restaurant or I'll begin to kill these hostages one by one," Rambo threatened. "Once your five minutes is up, I'll kill two hostages with each minute that passes!" He hung up the phone, walked over to his team, and proceeded to talk in a hushed tone.

"Hey assholes!" a muscular man spoke up. "Hey assholes!" he repeated.

Rambo slowly turned around and looked at the muscular man like he was crazy. "Something I can help you with?"

"Yeah, you and your crew real tough with those guns!" the muscular man barked. "Take these cuffs off me and I'll kick your ass up and down this ship!"

A smirk danced on Rambo's lips as he handed his rifle over to one of his comrades, then pulled a knife from the small of his back. Rambo slowly walked up to the muscular man. At first it looked like Rambo was about to stab the muscular man but, instead he cut the zip tie freeing the muscular man's hands from his back. Rambo walked back over to his comrade and handed him the knife, then turned his attention back to the muscular man. "You were saying?"

The muscular man swallowed hard. It was at that moment he knew he had made a huge mistake; a mistake that would more than likely cost him his life. "How about we talk about this like men?"

"I only see one man standing here," Rambo countered.

"Why don't you let all the women and kids go?" the muscular man suggested.

"If you beat me, I'll let all of the hostages go. How about that?" Rambo said.

The muscular man didn't really want to fight but, the rest of the hostages egged him on in hopes of him winning and them being let free. The muscular man took a deep breath and rushed towards Rambo with his fist balled up.

Rambo sidestepped the big man's attack landing a quick check hook in the process. He quickly followed up with a lightening quick three punch combination that left the muscular man stunned. The muscular man threw two wild haymakers. Rambo weaved the two punches easily and countered with a sharp elbow that landed flush on the muscular man's chin. Rambo then grabbed the muscular man and tossed him through the glass window sending him from one room into the next sending shattered glass flying everywhere. Rambo roughly grabbed the muscular man up to his feet, then landed six hard blows to the muscular man's face rearranging it in the process.

"That's enough!" a blonde hair woman yelled.

Rambo smiled as he watched the muscular man struggle to his feet. Rambo walked up the muscular man and stomped down on his kneecap knocking the bone out of place. The muscular man howled in pain as he clutched his knee. Rambo slid behind the muscular man and snapped his neck until a loud pop echoed loudly throughout the room.

Rambo made his way back to the room where the fight originated from. "Anyone else got something to say?!"

The brave blonde hair woman spoke up again. "That wasn't necessary!"

"Says who?"

"That man probably had a family! Shit we all have families!" the blonde hair woman yelled. "Do you not have a soul? You already have all of our money! What else do you want?"

Rambo smiled. "What's your name, sweetheart?"

"What the hell does it matter? All you going to do is kill us all anyway!"

Rambo walked back over to his fellow gunman, took his rifle back, and aimed it at the woman's face. "I asked you; what's your name?!"

"Do what you gotta do! I'm at peace with my God!" the blonde hair woman said in a strong tone.

Rambo pulled the trigger and blew the blonde hair woman's face off in cold blood and didn't even bat an eye. He quickly turned his gun on another man wearing glasses and shot him in the ear sending blood splattering on all the rest of the hostages. The rifle then landed on a pregnant woman. Rambo pulled down on the trigger and watched as the bullets riddled and rocked the pregnant woman's body from side to side.

Rambo quickly walked back over to the loud speaker and picked up the phone. "Three hostages are dead! Two more with each minute that passes!"

CHAPTER 19

Anthony Stone eased down the empty hall when he heard a voice come over the loud speaker announcing that every minute that passed, two hostages would be killed. Not knowing if Tasha would be one of the hostages that ended up losing her life, Stone hurried towards the restaurant.

The closer Stone made it towards the restaurant, he could hear a bunch of unnecessary yelling. He figured the gunmen were probably threatening all of the hostages keeping them slaves of fear. Stone peeked around the corner and saw a gunman blocking the entrance to the restaurant. The gunman also blocked Stone's vision making it difficult to see how many other gunmen were inside the restaurant.

Anthony Stone stood in his hiding spot as his brain began formulating a plan to rescue all the hostages. He looked up at the sky and noticed that it was now dark outside which meant that a S.W.A.T. team would soon be boarding the ship and opening fire on anyone who posed a threat. A loud series of gunshots snapped Stone out of his thoughts and back to reality.

***

Rambo glanced down at his watch and as soon as the seconds hand hit twelve, he violently snatched a woman up to her feet by her hair. "Get your ass up!" he growled forcefully shoving her into a wall where he opened fire riddling her body with bullets. "Who's next?" he asked looking out towards the rest of the hostages. Before anyone even got a chance to respond, Rambo violently grabbed a scrawny Chinese man by the back of his neck and flung him into the same wall as if he was a piece of trash. Immediately the man began begging for his life in his own language as tears ran down his face.

Rambo shook his head with a disgusted look on his face. "Be a fucking man for Christ sake!" With that being said, Rambo watched as the bullets from his rifle tore the Chinese man apart. Rambo walked back over to the phone and snatched it off the base, placing it to his ear. "Two more dead! You got sixty seconds to surrender or two more hostages will die!" He slammed the phone down. Rambo did a silent head count of his men and noticed the number kept getting lower and lower. Gathered in the restaurant were seven gunmen and about twenty other gunmen were out on the ship hunting the brave Samaritan down. The longer it took to find the fake tough guy running around the ship, the angrier Rambo became. He went to have a word with one of his soldiers when he heard a loud series of gunshots ring out followed by several of his men dropping to the ground.

CHAPTER 20

Once Anthony Stone heard Rambo's message over the loud speaker, he knew he had to make a move. He just hoped and prayed that Tasha wasn't one of the unfortunate hostages that lost their lives. On a silent count of three, Anthony Stone rounded the corner with a two handed grip on his rifle. He walked up on the gunman who stood in the doorway and shot him in the back of his head. Stone quickly entered the restaurant and turned his rifle on another one of the gunmen. He pulled the trigger and watched as the gunman's brains popped out the back of his skull. He turned his rifle on the next gunman and gunned him down as he tried to flee through a back door.

Rambo and two other gunmen returned fire as they scrambled for a place to hide and avoid the bullets from the A.R. 15.

Anthony Stone ran and slid across the floor as he gunned down two more gunmen. One of the gunmen took a bullet to the throat but, before he died, he managed to get a shot off and hit Stone in the shoulder.

"Arghh!" Stone growled as he aimed his rifle in Rambo's direction and squeezed down on the trigger. Rambo ran as a trail of bullets followed him. Rambo made a sharp cut and burst through a door that led to the kitchen as several bullets blew large holes through the door.

Anthony Stone quickly scrambled back to his feet, looking around making sure no more gunmen were around. Once he was sure the coast was clear, he pulled a knife from the small of his back. "HEY! LISTEN UP! I NEED EVERYONE'S ATTENTION REAL QUICK!" Anthony Stone yelled. "I'M GOING TO UNTIE ALL OF YOU BUT, WHEN I DO, IT'S EVERY MAN FOR HIMSELF! THIS SHIP HAS BEEN HIGH JACKED BY GUNMEN THAT ARE TERRORISTS WHO COULD CARE LESS IF YOU LIVE OR DIE! I URGE ALL OF YOU TO FIND A HIDING PLACE AND HIDE OR EITHER FIND A WEAPON AND DO WHAT YOU GOTTA DO!" As Stone spoke, he looked around hoping to see Tasha's face but, after looking over all of the hostages three times, he figured Tasha may have been one of the unfortunate hostages who lost their lives. It bothered him but, still the show must go on. Anthony Stone quickly untied all of the hostages and watched them all run out of the restaurant like chickens with their heads cut off. A few of the hostages removed the weapons from the dead gunmen before making their exit. Stone had no idea how this was going to play out but, he was just happy that he was at least able to free all of the hostages. As all of the hostages were running for their freedom, Stone glanced around one last time hoping his eyes would land on Tasha. He tried to keep a positive attitude after he wasn't able to locate Tasha in the mix of the crowd for the second time.

Anthony Stone slowly made his way towards the door that Rambo had ran through. He eased through the door with a two handed grip on his weapon making his way into the kitchen. Knowing that the S.W.A.T. team would be boarding the ship any second now, Stone had to move fast. He made a right turn pass the oven with the barrel of his rifle leading the way. When all of a sudden, a gunman appeared out of nowhere and slipped a plastic bag over Stone's face from behind. Out of natural instinct, Anthony Stone squeezed down on the trigger of his rifle sending a series of bullets up into the ceiling as he desperately tried to breath.

"Die you son of a bitch!" the gunman growled applying as much pressure as he could to the plastic bag. Anthony Stone was becoming a real pain in the ass and he planned on finally putting an end to him.

Stone dropped his rifle and grabbed at the plastic bag that was covering his face. He tried to pry an air hole in the bag but, the bag was too thick to penetrate. Stone back peddled slamming the gunman's back into the wall.

Bang!

He then raised his arm and came down hard jamming his elbow into the gunman's midsection. Anthony Stone delivered that same elbow three times in a row until the gunman finally released his grip on the plastic bag. Stone quickly ripped the bag from over his head and sucked in as much air as he possibly could. When suddenly, the gunman landed a powerful blow to his side, the same side that he had been stabbed in.

"Arghh!" Stone howled out in pain as the gunman picked him up and dumped him violently down on his head. The gunman climbed on top of Stone and delivered blow after blow to his face. Each blow he delivered had bad intentions. The gunman brutally beat Anthony Stone until he finally lost consciousness. The gunman pulled a large hunting knife from its holster and raised it over his head. Before he could bring his arm down, one of the newly freed hostages cracked the gunman over the back of his head with a pipe knocking him out cold. The man with the pipe beat the gunman repeatedly until he was sure that the gunman was officially dead. He then went to check on the brave man who had freed him along with all of the other hostages. He slapped Anthony Stone's face repeatedly until finally he began to stir.

Stone opened his eyes and immediately his hand shot out and gripped the man by the throat who was holding the pipe, assuming he was a threat.

The man quickly threw his hands up in surrender letting Anthony Stone know that he wasn't a threat. Stone slowly removed his hand from around the man's neck. "Thank you," Anthony Stone said in a raspy voice while he crawled back to his feet and grabbed his rifle from off the floor.

"It's the least I could do," the man said extending his hand. "Michael."

"Anthony," Stone replied as the two men shook hands. "So Michael, do you know how to defend yourself?"

Michael nodded his head in a yes motion. "Yeah."

Stone reached down and removed the gunman's .45 from his holster and handed it to Michael. "You're on your own. I have to find my girlfriend."

"Are you sure she's still alive?" Michael asked.

"God willing!"

CHAPTER 21

"We've been in this room long enough. I think it's time for us to make a move," Brett suggested seconds after a loud series of gunshots rang out.

"You think it's safe out there?" Tasha asked with a scared look on her face. Being trapped in the room and not being able to see anything was starting to play with Tasha's mind.

"The rest of the hostages could be getting freed right now and it would be a shame if we missed out because we're stuffed in this shitty ass room," Brett pointed out. "We'll, do it just how we did it earlier. You watch my back and I'll watch yours."

Tasha swallowed hard. Everything that Brett had said made sense but, it was the fear of the unknown that kept her feet cemented to the floor. "I need a weapon."

"Well the only way for you to get one is for us to leave this room and get one," Brett replied. "Besides it's dark outside now so that gives us more opportunities and places to hide but, we have to move now!"

Tasha didn't agree with the decision but, she figured she'd be safer with Brett than without him.

"Come on," Brett said leading the way out of the room. With it being night time, it made a big difference. There were more places to hide and a person was less likely to get spotted. Brett and Tasha eased their way down the hallway when a crazed looking man with a buzz hair cut sprung from around the corner carrying a pipe in a threatening manner. Brett quickly raised his weapon and put the man with the buzz cut down before he had the opportunity to hurt him or Tasha. After further inspection, Tasha recognized the dead man with the buzz cut. "He was one of the hostages locked up with us," she pointed out.

Brett looked up and saw three woman running blindly down the hallway looking for a place to hide. "Looks like someone freed all of the hostages," he said turning his gaze on Tasha. "Probably your boyfriend Anthony Stone."

Tasha looked up at Brett. "You think so?"

"Who else do you know who could have freed those hostages?" Brett asked with a raised brow.

"If Anthony is still alive, we have to find him," Tasha said with excitement in her voice. With all the gunshots she'd heard in the last hour, she prayed that Anthony Stone wasn't hurt and if he was, she prayed that he wasn't hurt too bad to where it was life threatening.

"Where do we start?"

"I have no idea," Tasha admitted as she noticed four more hostages run pass them. With all of the hostages running around freely, it was going to make it that much harder to find Anthony Stone. Tasha and Brett turned the corner and saw a gunman shoot down four hostages who were running for their lives. As the gunman turned his back, two other hostages crept up on him from behind and beat him down with chains and sticks until the gunman was no longer breathing.

"It's too dangerous out here," Brett said as he grabbed Tasha's hand and led her in the opposite direction. They jogged down the hall and stopped when they saw two more hostages standing at the end of the hall with mean looks on their faces and sticks in their hands. Brett and Tasha's jogging turned into a fast walk, then they completely stopped.

Brett raised his hands in surrender. "Hey, we're all on the same team!" he called out to the couple who stood only a few yards away. The couple didn't respond. "Did you hear me? I said we're all on the same team!"

The couple didn't respond, instead they began walking slowly in Brett and Tasha's direction with the look of violence dancing in their eyes. Immediately Brett raised his rifle. "Get back!" he warned. "I'm not playing! I will blow the both of you out of your shoes!" The couple ignored the threats and continued moving forward. Brett squeezed the trigger on the rifle.

CLICK! CLICK! CLICK!

"What the fuck?!" Brett said looking down at the weapon in his hands. He had picked the wrong time to run out of bullets. He looked up and the couple yelled as they charged them.

The male hostage swung the stick with extreme force. The blow was intended to knock Brett out cold but, just before the stick landed, Brett raised his arm and the stick shattered over his forearm. Brett quickly grabbed the hostage as the two men went crashing violently through one of the room doors. Brett landed on top of the hostage and landed four strong blows to the man's head that put him out. Brett stood to his feet and snatched the sheets off the bed and quickly used them to tie the hostage's hands behind his back before he regained consciousness.

Meanwhile, outside of the room, the female hostage charged Tasha swinging a stick with great force. Tasha went low, ducked the stick strike and, scooped the female hostage's legs from under her dumping her on her head. The female hostage hit the floor hard and flipped Tasha over in the process landing on top of her. The female hostage wrapped her hands around Tasha's neck and began to squeeze with all of her might. "DIE YOU BITCH!" she growled as spittle flew from her mouth landing on Tasha's face. Tasha grabbed the female hostage's hands trying to pry them from around her neck but, the woman's grip was just too tight. Just as Tasha's eyes were about to close due to lack of air, she saw Brett standing over the female hostage's shoulders holding a foreign object in his hand.

Brett hit the woman over the head with a metal pipe. He watched as the woman's body tumbled over and blood leaked from her head like a faucet. "You

okay?!" he asked extending his hand, helping Tasha
back up to her feet.

"Thank you," Tasha said brushing herself off.
She didn't understand why the hostages were trying
to kill her and Brett. "What the hell is going on?"
Tasha asked. "Why are they trying to kill us?"

"Someone must have freed the hostages and from
the looks of it, they don't know who's, who so I guess
it's every man and woman for themselves," Brett
explained.

"This is going to get ugly," Tasha said to no one
in particular. Numerous gunmen and thousands of
hostages running around killing each other was a
recipe for disaster. As Tasha and Brett stood there
having a discussion, all of the lights on the ship
suddenly went out.

"Shit!" Brett cursed as loud screams and
gunshots filled the air.

CHAPTER 22

Agent Mark Wiggins sat on the helicopter with a serious look on his face. He was the squad leader of the S.W.A.T. team that was being sent onto the ship to kill all of the gunmen and anyone else who stood in their way. Mark Wiggins' job was to eliminate all of the gunmen and to do it in a quick manner before the media caught wind of the story and what was really going down on the ship. Mark was one of the best agents in the world and he only got called for the big jobs and tonight was no different. Mark had personally handpicked ten of his best men to join him on this mission, men that he knew had no problem killing. "Cut the lights off on the ship," Mark ordered. He and all of his men were dressed in scuba gear. With all of the lights on the ship off, it would make it easier for the S.W.A.T. team to board the ship undetected. "All we know is there are close to four thousand hostages onboard the ship. We're not sure how many gunmen are on board but, if I had to guess, I would say around forty to fifty," Mark said in an even tone. "Alright boys, let's go have some fun!"

The helicopter stood stationary while the S.W.A.T. team got all of their gear together and prepared to jump. The ten-man team jumped off the helicopter two at a time down into the ocean. Agent Mark Wiggins plowed into the water and immediately the flashlight attached to his goggles turned on making it easy for him to see under water. Mark and his team were approximately the length of a football field away from the ship. Mark and his team swam under water in a perfect diamond formation. While swimming, Mark planned in his mind how this entire mission was going to play out. He was prepared to do whatever it took to complete this mission. Mark was a trained killing machine and he knew he was the best in the business. When Mark and his team reached the ship, they all removed a rifle, aimed it at the ship and pulled the trigger. A large hook shot out of the rifle landing on the boat hooking onto something solid. The hook had a rope connected to it. Mark and his team quietly climbed aboard the ship and stepped out of their scuba gear. Underneath the scuba gear, the S.W.A.T. team was dressed in all black army gear and they were all ready to go to war! Mark pulled his night vision goggles down over his eyes and cut them on. Immediately his vision turned lime green, making it easy for him and his team to see in the dark as they moved throughout the ship. Two hostages came running around the corner with scared looks on their faces. Mark wasted no time putting the two potential threats down with head shots. Him and his team stepped over the bodies as if they weren't there and continued on throughout the ship. Mark stopped in the middle of his tracks when he heard a loud commotion coming from up ahead and around the corner. With hand signals, Mark signaled for half of his team to go downstairs while he and the other half took care of the upstairs.

Mark and his team rounded the corner and saw four men standing over two men beating the bodies repeatedly with sticks. He suspected that those were hostages beating on two gunmen but, in all reality he had no way of knowing who was who on the dark ship. Mark Wiggins and his team quietly snuck up on the group. Before anyone could figure out what was going on, Mark's team put the entire group down with accurate head shots.

Thwap! Thwap! Thwap! Thwap!

With silenced weapons, Mark and his team moved throughout the ship like ghost. As they continued on throughout the ship, Mark and his team walked up on four guys running around the corner. Once the saw the guns pointed in their direction, the foursome immediately threw their hands up in surrender. "Please don't shoot!" one of the hostages yelled. "Please help us!"

"GET ON THE FLOOR AND PLACE YOUR HANDS BEHIND YOUR HEAD!" Mark yelled with his rifle held steady, finger wrapped around the trigger, and ready to fire. The foursome did as they were told. Mark quickly tied each of the foursome's hands behind their back with a zip tie. Any hostages that surrendered themselves would be zip tied while all the others would be shot down and killed. As Mark Wiggins moved on to the next hostage to zip tie them, he spotted a gunman behind his men.

"GET DOWN!" Mark yelled as he quickly dived out of the way as the bullets started to fly. The gunman shot two of Mark's men before disappearing into the darkness.

"SHIT!" Mark yelled kneeling down next to one of his wounded comrades checking to see how much damage had been done. The fellow agent had a gaping hole in the side of his neck and was already gargling on his own blood. Mark held his fellow soldier's hand until he took his last breath. Mark let the soldier's hand go when two of his men opened fire just over his head gunning down three men who were carrying knives. Things on the ship were worse than Mark had anticipated but, he was still confident that he and his men could get the job done. "Stay in formation fellas!" Mark Wiggins ordered.

Mark continued down the hall as him and his team eased their way up on a utility closet. Team captain number two and three flanked both sides of the door while Mark stood in the middle. Mark gave the signal and team captain number two snatched the door open. Mark's eyes lit up as he got ready to pull the trigger but, then eased his finger off the trigger when he saw around ten to twelve hostages hiding in the utility closet. "MY NAME IS AGENT MARK WIGGINS AND WE'RE HERE TO HELP!" he yelled. "I NEED ALL OF YOU TO LAY ON THE FLOOR AND PUT YOUR HANDS BEHIND YOUR HEAD!" Mark watched carefully as his team zip tied the hostage's hands behind their back and gently sat them on the floor. "We have to rescue the rest of the hostages and we'll be back for you," Mark told the hostages as him and his team entered the restaurant where the hostages were originally being held. They silently moved from the restaurant, to the kitchen, and then to the gymnasium next door. Mark placed his ear up against the door and he could hear movement inside and what sounded like feet shuffling on the other side of the door. On a silent count of three, he snatched the door open and tossed two cans of tear gas inside then quickly shut the door. Two minutes later, Mark and his team entered the gymnasium and zip tied all of the hostage's hands behind their backs. Mark noticed two men in army gear and figured they were gunmen so without thinking twice, he put a bullet in both of their heads.

CHAPTER 23

Anthony Stone eased through the ship with a firm grip on his rifle. When all of the lights went out, it made it damn near impossible to see, especially if someone was trying to creep up on you from behind. His plan was to search for Tasha in hopes of finding her but, now his entire thought process had changed. Now all Stone wanted to do was find a way to stay alive until sunrise. He tip toed throughout the ship looking for a good place to hide until sunrise but, instead of finding a hiding spot, Stone found six men around the corner. These weren't just ordinary men, these men held metal pipes in their hands and had a kill or be killed look in their eyes. Stone aimed his rifle at the pack of men. "Listen fellas," he began in a neutral tone. "We're all on the same team here guys. What do you say, y'all put those pipes down?" He said trying to avoid having to take six innocent lives. "I'll even lower my weapon first," Stone said slowly lowering his weapon but, still holding it in a way where if he needed to, he would still be able to fire it at will.

The leader of the pack, a black guy with a baby afro stopped a few feet away from the Detective and a smirk appeared on his face. "Yo, this is the dude who helped us out of the restaurant." With that being said, all of the six men lowered their weapons. "We appreciate what you did for us back there," the baby afro guy said extending his hand.

Anthony Stone shook the guy's hand as a loud series of gunshots rang out. Bullets tore through four of the six men standing in front of Stone. "GET

DOWN!" Stone yelled as he dropped down to the floor and played dead. Two gunmen walked up and gunned down the remaining two hostages like they were shooting at a target at the shooting range.

Stone laid on the floor holding his breath pretending to be dead. Once he heard the footsteps get close enough, he sat up and shot the first gunman in the face. Before the gunman's body could even hit the floor, Stone had turned his rifle on the second gunman and blew half of his face off. Stone made it to his feet and removed the 9mm from the holster of one of the dead gunmen. Anthony Stone looked up and saw five men turn the corner dressed in S.W.A.T. gear. "Shit!" he cursed as he burst through the staircase door as a trail of silenced bullets followed his every move until the staircase door closed behind him. Stone picked himself up off the floor. He knew it wouldn't be long before a S.W.A.T. team boarded the ship to try and tame the situation. Stone ran through the next door as he heard the door to the staircase get snatched open. Stone didn't want to have to kill any of the agents on the S.W.A.T. team but, in order for him to stay alive, it was looking like that would be his only option. Stone ran through the area made for the comedy club and hid behind a row of seats. He propped the barrel of his rifle up on one of the seats and waited. Anthony Stone squeezed half way down on the trigger in anticipation of the S.W.A.T. team to come bursting through the door. Approximately fifteen seconds later, the door swung open and the first two S.W.A.T. members that entered the comedy club, Anthony Stone sent them right back out the same way they came in with shots to their chest and neck area. "I'M A COP!" he yelled. "I'M GOING TO SURRENDER!" No response! Twenty seconds later, two stun grenades came flying into the comedy club. "Shit!" Stone cursed as he took off in a sprint but, it was too late. The blast knocked him off of his feet. Stone hit the floor. His ears were ringing nonstop, his vision was blurry, and it felt like he was in the middle of a fog moving in slow motion.

The remaining three S.W.A.T. agents ran inside the comedy club with their weapons drawn ready to fire at will. They ran through the comedy club looking for their target when the door to the other entrance burst open and Rambo and another gunman stormed through door. When Rambo ran into the S.W.A.T. team, a smirk danced on his lips.

"FUCK YOU, PIGS!" Rambo growled as him and his comrade opened fire on the S.W.A.T. team. The S.W.A.T. team quickly took cover and returned fire.

Anthony Stone crawled on his hands and knees trying to shake off the cobwebs. When his vision finally cleared up, Stone saw two gunmen having a serious shootout with the S.W.A.T. team. Stone looked down for a second to locate his rifle and when he looked back up, he saw the last remaining S.W.A.T. members laying on the ground gasping for air.

Rambo noticed Anthony Stone lying on the floor struggling to make it back to his feet. "Look what we have here," he said to his fellow gunman. When Rambo didn't get a response, he looked over his shoulder and saw his partner lying face down on the floor in a puddle of blood piled directly under his face. "SHIT!" Rambo cursed turning his attention back on Anthony Stone. "So you're the clown that's been causing all of this trouble," he chuckled as he tossed his rifle down to the floor and roughly grabbed Stone by the back of his neck. "I'm going to kill you with my bare hands and I'm going to enjoy every second of it," he said then violently slammed Stone down into the floor.

CHAPTER 24

Rambo roughly grabbed Anthony Stone again, pulling him to his feet. Stone took a swing but, Rambo blocked the blow with ease and delivered a knee to Stone's midsection followed up with a hard elbow to the middle of his back sending him hard down to the floor. "FIGHT BACK!" Rambo yelled as he stomped down on Anthony Stone's lower back. Stone crawled back up to his feet and stumbled a bit. His equilibrium was still a little bit off from the previous explosion. Stone threw a wild haymaker that Rambo ducked easily and came back up with an uppercut that dropped Anthony Stone on his back. Stone made it back to his feet and he could see clear now. That last blow to the head shook the cobwebs loose. Stone threw a quick jab that Rambo blocked but, it distracted him enough so Stone was able to land a sweeping right hook that connected with Rambo's chin. Stone ran into Rambo and rushed him, forcing them both to flip over a row of chairs. Anthony Stone kicked Rambo in the face and then stood to his feet. Rambo got up and threw a quick four punch combo. Stone blocked all four punches while stepping back but, wasn't quick enough to block the kick that bounced off the side of his head. Rambo grabbed Stone in a grapple and went for a takedown. Anthony Stone went low blocking the take down attempt and then delivered two blows to the back of Rambo's head. The two men rolled around on the floor giving as much as they could give. Both men made it back to their feet and Rambo delivered a side kick to the pit of Stone's stomach sending him sliding across the floor. Rambo reached down, grabbed Stone by the ankles, and violently swung him into the wall. Rambo snatched Anthony Stone back up to his feet and wrapped his hands around his throat. He squeezed until Stone's eyes began to roll into the back of his head. A smile appeared on Rambo's face when he saw Stone fading out. Rambo applied even more pressure when he heard a voice coming from behind.

Standing behind Rambo stood Brett and Tasha. Brett aimed his rifle at Rambo. "LET HIM GO NOW!" Brett warned.

"What the hell are you doing?" Rambo asked with a mean look on his face.

"I SAID, LET HIM GO NOW!" Brett yelled taking a step closer. Rambo finally released his grip from around Anthony Stone's throat and tossed him down to the floor. "Now what?" Rambo asked.

Without warning, Brett pulled the trigger and shot half of Rambo's face off. He stood over Rambo's body and fired four more shots into the gunman's face making sure he was dead.

Immediately, Tasha ran over to Anthony Stone's aid. "Baby are you okay?" she asked as tears rolled down her face. It hurt her to see her man in the condition he was in but, at the same time, she was thankful that he was still alive. "ANTHONY, TALK TO ME!" she yelled.

"Hey baby," Stone said in a raspy tone as he flashed a smile. Tasha smiled as she tried to hug all the air out of his body.

Brett walked up, extended his hand, and helped Anthony Stone up to his feet. "Nice to finally meet you. I'm Brett," he said extending his hand again.

"Detective Anthony Stone," he replied as the two men shook hands.

"Brett here, kept me alive," Tasha volunteered.

Anthony Stone nodded. "Thank you Brett! I appreciate you!"

"Thank me later," Brett said. "How do we get out of here? With all these hostages running around like crazy, it's not too safe around here."

"We have to get back to the restaurant and make an announcement on the loud speaker," Anthony

Stone said. "And pray that we don't run into anymore gunmen or S.W.A.T. members."

Brett and Tasha both placed one of Anthony Stone's arms around their necks and helped assist him as they all headed for the restaurant.

The trio exited the comedy club and entered the staircase. They had to go up three flights to get to the restaurant. "I got it," Stone said when they made it to the first flight. The trio made their way up the stairs when the door burst open on the level above them and three hostages charged the trio. Brett shot the first hostage in the gut as the second hostage tackled Brett sending them both violently tumbling down the stairs. The last hostage swung on Anthony Stone. He easily blocked the blow and swung the hostage into the wall, then wrestled the man down to the floor. "Hey, we're the good guys!" Anthony Stone barked. "Stop fighting and I'm going to let you up!" Once the man stopped putting up a fight, Stone let him up.

"HEY, THESE ARE THE GOOD GUYS!" the hostage yelled to his other friend who was in the process of choking Brett out.

"THE GOOD GUYS?!" the man repeated from the bottom of the stairs with his fist raised in mid swing. The two hostages quickly helped Brett back up to his feet. "Sorry about that," the hostage apologized.

"Come on, we're heading to the restaurant so we can make an announcement to let all the hostages know to meet back in the restaurant," Stone explained as they all continued to the restaurant.

On their way to the restaurant, Anthony Stone and his crew stepped over so many dead bodies that Tasha threw up two times before they finally reached the restaurant. On the way, they all managed to find a firearm to protect themselves.

When they reached the restaurant, Stone grabbed the phone off the wall and spoke directly into the receiver. "Attention, this is Detective Anthony Stone speaking. I need all hostages to report back to the restaurant. I'm here with several other hostages and we're all armed and will protect you. Again, I need all hostages to report back to the restaurant. Anyone not in the restaurant will be ruled as a terrorist."

CHAPTER 25

Mark Wiggins and his team gunned down several hostages on their way to the control center on the ship. So far he and his team had killed at least a hundred and thirty people that included men and women. Mark had a job to do and he planned on completing the mission by any means necessary. Mark led the way towards the control center, when he and his team heard footsteps coming from behind them. Mark spun around and watched as a gunman gunned down two of his fellow agents. Mark Wiggins took a bullet to the chest as he managed to get off a shot of his own that managed to blow the gunman's ear off. The gunman stumbled backwards, dropped his weapon, and then took off around the corner. Mark climbed back to his feet and took off after the gunman. Mark turned the corner, stood wide legged, and aimed his rifle at the moving target. He waited until he had a clear shot before he pulled the trigger, dropping the fleeing gunman in his tracks. Mark Wiggins lowered his rifle when an arm slipped around his neck from behind.

A hostage managed to slip behind Mark and put him in a chokehold. Mark Wiggins pushed backwards ramming the hostage's back up against the wall forcing the hostage to release the grip around his neck. Mark spun around and landed a four punch combo to the man's face, then violently snapped the man's neck, and watched him fall down to the floor. A screaming woman charged Mark with a metal pipe in her hand. He ducked the pipe and flipped the woman over his shoulders sending her overboard.

He heard the woman's body splash loudly in the ocean as two more hostages charged him. Mark Wiggins removed a five-inch knife from a holster attached to his wrist. He cut the first hostage six times before he even realized he had been cut. He then moved on to the next hostage and uppercut him with the knife jamming it under the man's chin killing him instantly. Mark went back to the first hostage and landed a kick that bounced off the man's head knocking him out cold. Mark kneeled down and viciously snapped the man's neck. He wasn't taking any chances. He pulled a backup Five-Seven pistol from his leg holster and continued towards the command center.

During his scuffle, Mark Wiggins lost his night vision goggles. Having no other choice, Mark pulled a small Maglite from the small of his back. He held his weapon with one hand and the Maglite with his other hand. Mark used the light from the Maglite to lead him through the ship. His flashlight led him around the corner and then up a small flight of stairs. Mark Wiggins turned the Maglite off when he reached the control center and heard loud talking coming from up ahead. He crept towards the door, then on a silent count of three, he snatched the door open.

CHAPTER 26

Inside the control center stood three gunmen armed with assault rifles. Standing in the middle of the control center rested the Captain of the ship along with his entire staff. The three gunmen enjoyed a nice laugh when the door burst open and a man dressed in all black entered the room.

Mark stepped in the control center and fired three shots, then kept a firm two handed grip on his weapon. With his pin point accuracy, Mark was able to hit all three of the gunmen with headshots killing them right where they stood.

Mark holstered his weapon, walked over to the controls, and turned the ship back in the opposite direction. Mark pulled his burner phone out and dialed a number, then placed it up to his ear. "Yeah, I turned the ship around and it's headed to the nearest dock. Have a team and several ambulances on standby. Several of my men didn't make it." He paused for a second. "For all I know, it's just me left...No, I haven't laid eyes on Anthony Stone as of yet...Will do sir." Mark Wiggins ended the call and slipped the phone back down in a small compartment in his pants. He pulled his Five-Seven pistol from his holster when he heard an announcement from Detective Anthony Stone over the loud speaker informing all of the hostages to make their way back to the restaurant. Mark Wiggins walked over and glanced at the ship's layout and quickly figured out where the restaurant was located. Mark pulled out his Maglite and headed for the restaurant. He slowly made his way down the stairs when three hostages ran by him at a quick pace. Mark quickly bent around the corner and dropped the three hostages. He wasn't in the business of taking chancing with his life so anyone who posed or looked like they could pose a threat was going to be fired on. As Mark walked towards the restaurant he heard several footsteps coming from all different directions. Two more hostages darted around the corner and he wasted no time putting a bullet in both of their backs. A third hostage rounded the corner and stopped dead in her tracks, raising her hands in surrender. "Please don't shoot!" the woman pleaded.

"DOWN ON THE FLOOR NOW!" Mark Wiggins yelled with his gun pointed at the woman's forehead. Once the woman was on the floor, he quickly zip tied her hands behind her back. He looked up and saw several hostages round the corner. Once they spotted the gunman dressed in all black, they all quickly split up and scattered in different directions. Mark ignored them and continued on towards the restaurant.

CHAPTER 27

Anthony Stone and Brett helped all of the hostages through the doors of the restaurant. A few of the hostages were a little skeptical about heading back to the same spot where they were just being held captive earlier. "We're here to help!" Anthony Stone announced as all of the hostages began to emerge from their hiding spots and head to the restaurant. Stone craned his neck and looked back to make sure Tasha was okay. He smiled when she gave him a thumbs up. Over on the other side of the room, Tasha helped a few wounded women get comfortable and assured them that everything was going to be alright. "Help is on the way, so you have nothing to worry about."

"Are there anymore gunmen still on board this ship?" another woman asked with a look of concern on her face.

"No we are all safe now Sweety," Tasha said flashing a friendly smile. The hostages as well as Tasha had been through a lot ever since they boarded the ship so she understood why some of the passengers were a little skeptical.

***

Anthony Stone helped escort a few of the hostages inside the restaurant when he saw a man about twenty yards away laid out on the floor moaning like a wounded animal. "Hey Brett," Anthony Stone called out. "We have a wounded man at twelve o'clock," he nodded in the direction of the body. "Look over the hostages. I'll be right back," Stone said pulling his 9mm from his waistband and heading over towards the wounded man. He made sure he moved with caution just in case this was a setup. When Anthony Stone reached the wounded man, he realized it was a S.W.A.T. agent that was on the receiving end of a bullet.

"He...he...help me," the agent moaned. From the tone of his voice, Anthony Stone could tell that the agent was in pain.

"Where are you hit?"

"Took one to the side of the neck," the agent murmured. Anthony Stone stuck his 9mm back in his waistband and helped the agent up to his feet, then tossed him over his shoulder and carried him back to the restaurant army style. As Anthony Stone carried the wounded agent he felt movement. The

S.W.A.T. agent removed a knife from his holster and attempted to cut Anthony Stone's throat.

Having no other choice, Stone grabbed the blade of the knife to keep from getting his throat slit. The knife cut up Anthony Stone's hand as he held a tight grip on the blade. Blood ran down Stone's wrist as he struggled with the agent before finally tossing the agent over board.

Brett peeked his head out the door and watched as Anthony Stone tossed the wounded man overboard. He quickly jetted out of the restaurant and ran to Stone's aid.

"Hey, you alright?" Brett asked with a gun in his hand.

"Yeah, asshole tried to kill me!"

"Who was that guy?" Brett asked. "He didn't look like one of the regular gunmen."

"S.W.A.T.," Anthony Stone replied quickly.

"Why would S.W.A.T. come onboard to try and kill us?" Brett asked with a confused look on his face.

"Sacrifice a little to save a lot," Anthony Stone said shaking his head. "I don't agree with the way they do things but, hey who am I to tell them how to run their show?"

"We need more good cops like yourself on the streets," Brett said.

"Did you notice that the ship has turned around?"

"Yes, I did notice. I thought you did that," Brett said with a raised brow. "You did do that, right?"

"Wasn't me," Stone answered. "That means there's still someone else on this ship so keep your eyes open because I don't know who this person is; could be another S.W.A.T. member," he pointed out.

"I have a bad feeling about us being out here," Brett admitted. "Let's get back inside the restaurant."

Anthony Stone looked over his shoulder and saw a man dressed in all black quickly trotting towards the restaurant. "Hey, stay on point. We got company." Stone looked out and noticed the man was wearing S.W.A.T. gear and pulled his weapon from his waistband. "HEY!" he called out to the S.W.A.T. member. Stone and Brett quickly ducked down when the S.W.A.T. agent fired three shots in their direction.

CHAPTER 28

Captain Fisher stood over to the side pacing back and forth. Every few seconds, he made sure to glance down at his watch. He knew that the S.W.A.T. team had boarded the ship by now and just hoped that things weren't getting out of hand on that ship, especially with all of the hostages on board. Captain Fisher knew Anthony Stone could hold his own, he just worried about the S.W.A.T. team mistaking him for a gun toting terrorist and gunning him down in the process. Captain Fisher pulled out a cigarette, placed it between his lips, and lit it up. His cell phone was glued to his hand just in case Detective Stone by chance decided to call.

"Are you okay? You look like you're about to shit a brick!" the Lieutenant said playfully. "Why don't you sit down and relax?"

"Can't relax while one of my men is on board that shit," Captain Fisher said taking a long drag from his cigarette and letting the smoke blow out of his nose. "Have you heard anything from the S.W.A.T. team?"

"Yes, Agent Mark Wiggins radioed in and so far everything is going according to plan," the Lieutenant said with a smile.

"How long ago was that sir?"

"About an hour ago," said the Lieutenant.

"Did he say if the hostages were safe?"

The Lieutenant shook his head. "No but, I gave him a specific order to get that ship back however he had to before the media catches wind of this fiasco."

"But sir what about the hostages?" Captain Fisher asked with his voice full of concern.

153

"I feel bad for the hostages too but, S.W.A.T. has to do what they have to do," the Lieutenant said coldly. "I'm all about results!"

"I understand that Lieutenant but, what I'm trying to say is...."

"Listen!" the Lieutenant cut him off. "I could give a shit about those hostages! All I care about is getting that ship back in one piece and my team killing The Genius and the rest of those terrorist on that ship!"

Just as Captain Fisher was about to reply, he heard his phone ring. "Detective Stone tell me something good," he answered quickly.

"All of the gunmen on the ship are dead and the ship is headed back in your direction," Anthony Stone explained.

"That's great!" Captain Fisher said with a smile. "I knew you could do it."

"Thanks Captain but, we still have a problem."

"What?"

"We have a member from the S.W.A.T. firing on me and innocent hostages," Anthony Stone explained. "And I identified myself."

Captain Fisher covered the receiver and looked over to the Lieutenant. "Hey, my man says one of your S.W.A.T. guys are firing on him and innocent hostages after he identified himself," Captain Fisher explained. "All of the gunmen are dead and the ship is headed back this way. Call your man and tell him to stand down now!"

"No can do," the Lieutenant said with a smirk on his face. "My team is on that ship and if they're firing on anyone, I'm sure they have a good reason and I trust my men."

"YOU PIECE OF SHIT!" Captain Fisher growled as he charged the Lieutenant and tackled him down to the ground, climbed on top of him, and began raining punches down on the Lieutenant's face until a gang of cops pulled him off of the now bloodied Lieutenant.

The Lieutenant sat up and flashed a bloody smile. "You'll never work in law enforcement ever again! You can kiss your career goodbye!"

"FUCK YOU!" Captain Fisher yelled then went and picked his phone up from off the ground and placed it back up to his ear. "Stone, you still there?"

"Yeah Captain I'm here. Let me know what you want me to do."

"Do whatever you have to do," Captain Fisher said. "Just make it back in one piece."

CHAPTER 29

Anthony Stone hung up the phone then looked over towards Brett. "Looks like we're on our own until this ship reaches its destination."

"Don't worry, I got your back," Brett assured him.

Stone didn't know what the S.W.A.T. guy's problem was but, he couldn't allow him to harm him nor any of the innocent hostages even if it meant losing his own life. "Hey, I need you to watch the front door and I'll watch the back," he called out to Brett.

"Baby is everything okay?" Tasha asked sensing that something was wrong.

"Yes, we have one more gunman outside from the S.W.A.T. team."

"I thought S.W.A.T. were supposed to be the good guys?" Tasha said with a confused looked on her face.

Anthony Stone shrugged. "I did too. I don't know what this guy's problem is and quite frankly, I don't give a damn."

Stone ordered all of the hostages to stay away from the windows and to stay low at all times. He knew whoever the gunman outside of the restaurant was, he was well trained and ready for action.

***

Agent Mark Wiggins crept towards the restaurant but, he would more than likely he would be shot trying to enter through the front door so he had to find another way inside. He looked up and saw a metal ladder attached to the side of the building. Without thinking twice, Mark jumped, grabbed the ladder, and proceeded to climb to the roof when he felt a slight vibration on his hip notifying him that the Lieutenant was trying to get in touch with him via radio. Mark grabbed his walkie-talkie, pressed the button, and spoke into it. "Yeah."

"What the hell is going on, on that ship?" the Lieutenant asked.

"Business as usual," Mark replied in a dry tone.

"I got a call saying you are firing on innocent hostages and a Detective who identified himself. What the hell is going on?!" The Lieutenant asked.

"This so called Detective killed one of my men and tossed him overboard," Mark Wiggins said in a harsh whisper. "I'm not stopping until he's dead!"

"Listen Mark, stand down; that's an order! You hear me!?" the Lieutenant asked.

Mark Wiggins tossed his walkie-talkie out into the ocean ignoring everything the Lieutenant had just told him. For Mark this situation was no longer business, it was now personal. He had just witnessed one of his best friends get tossed overboard. Now he was going to have to explain to his friend's wife why her husband was no longer alive and why her kids no longer had a father. Mark knew when the mission was over that he would more than likely be suspended or even fired for his actions but, at that very moment, he could care less. He walked gently on the roof as he screwed a silencer on the barrel of his Five-Seven pistol. He aimed his pistol down at the roof and opened fire.

CHAPTER 30

"EVERYONE SETTLE DOWN," Anthony Stone yelled out to the crowd of hostages. "I PROMIESE THIS WILL BE ALL OVER WITH, REAL SOON! I JUST NEED EVERYONE TO REMAIN CALM!"

"Forget this shit!" A male hostage barked standing to his feet. "My wife and I are hungry and I'm going to find us some food! She's pregnant!"

"Listen brother, I'll find some food for your wife. I just need you to have a seat and relax," Anthony Stone said in a calm tone.

"Absolutely not!" the man growled. "I'll relax when my wife and unborn child has some food in their stomachs!" The man headed for the back door when his head violently jerked back and his body collapsed to the floor.

Anthony Stone looked on in horror as shots came through the ceiling killing several hostages. Without thinking twice, Stone raised his rifle up to the ceiling and squeezed down on the trigger. He let go of the trigger and stared up at the ceiling hoping one of his bullets hit the gunman. Stone and Brett both opened fire on the ceiling when they heard the sound of footsteps running across the ceiling.

"EVERYBODY GET DOWN!" Anthony Stone yelled never taking his eyes off of the ceiling. Brett looked up at the ceiling as three more hostages dropped down to the floor.

Stone ran out the front door since he knew that the gunman was up on the roof. He looked from left to right and spotted a ladder attached to the side of the building. He jumped up, grabbed the ladder, and pulled himself up to the roof. When he reached the roof, he immediately spotted the gunman.

"DROP YOUR WEAPON NOW!" Anthony Stone yelled with his rifle trained on the gunman.

"YOU KILLED MY FRIEND!" Mark Wiggins growled looking his friend's killer in the eyes.

"AND I'M GOING TO KILL YOU TOO, IF YOU DON'T PUT DOWN THAT GUN!" Stone warned with his finger pressed halfway down on the trigger.

Mark stared at Anthony Stone long and hard, then aimed his rifle down at the roof and squeezed down on the trigger until he fell through the roof down into the restaurant. Stone quickly ran over to the hole in the roof and looked down into the restaurant.

Mark quickly scrambled to his feet and tackled Brett down to the floor.

"SHIT!" Anthony Stone cursed as he jumped from the roof landing down into the restaurant. He raised his rifle but, didn't have a clear shot with the gunman and Brett both tussling for possession of the rifle.

Brett kneed the gunman in the groin, then managed to overpower the gunman for possession of the rifle. Brett pointed the rifle at the gunman's face as his hands shook uncontrollably.

"Don't do it Brett! He's not worth it!" Anthony Stone placed a friendly hand on Brett's shoulder.

"I'm going to kill both of you cocksuckers!" Mark growled with fire dancing in his eyes. "You better kill me now because if you don't, I'm going to kill the both of you with my bare hands."

Stone reached down and slapped the taste out of Mark's mouth. "SHUT THE HELL UP!" he yelled tired of hearing the man's voice.

"Put that gun down and let's do this the old fashion way," Mark said slowly standing to his feet and cracked his neck.

Stone was about to put his weapon down and accept the gunman's challenge when he felt Tasha's hand gently touch his lower back.

"It's over baby," Tasha said in a soft tone. "You saved all of us. You have nothing else to prove."

Anthony Stone and Mark Wiggins had a staring contest while Tasha's words went in one ear and out the other. "Here baby, hold this for me for a second," Anthony Stone said handing her his rifle. Tasha knew what that look in her man's eyes meant. That look meant that his mind was already made up so instead of arguing with him, she slowly removed the rifle from his hand as everyone stepped back giving the two men room to get busy.

CHAPTER 31

Anthony Stone took a fighting stance as the room got extremely quiet anticipating the action that they knew was about to come. Mark Wiggins broke the silence as he ran and charged Stone throwing punches with both hands. Stone blocked all the punches with ease and then landed a right cross of his own. Stone got on his toes and bounced around. Immediately he could tell that his movements were throwing the gunman off. Stone jumped in, landed two punches to Mark's face, and then jumped right back out. Mark knew he couldn't beat Stone straight up so he had to figure out a way to turn this into a dirty fight. Mark moved in and took two punches just so he could land one. The one punch he landed hit Stone right on his side where he had been stabbed.

"Arggh!" Stone howled doubling over in pain. He held his side as Mark landed two punches that bounced off the side of his head. The two blows stunned Stone causing him to wobble back into the wall.

Mark ran, jumped in the air, and kneed Anthony Stone in the chest. Stone dropped down to his hands and knees as he struggled to suck in air. His chest felt like it had literally been caved in. Mark roughly grabbed Stone, shoved his head between his legs, and power bombed the Detective down to the unforgiving floor.

Tasha covered her eyes. She could no longer watch her man take a beating like this.

Mark pulled Stone back to his feet and threw a powerful uppercut. Stone weaved the uppercut and swept Mark's legs from under him. The men quickly raced back to their feet. Stone managed to beat Mark to the punch and slip behind him where he put the man in a deadly choke hold.

Mark's eyes grew wide when he felt his oxygen being cut off. He made an attempt to scratch Anthony Stone's eyes out and ram his back into the wall. The more Mark moved around, the more pressure Stone applied.

Anthony Stone didn't let up until the gunman was no longer moving. Once Stone was sure the gunman was out cold, he snapped his neck in a quick motion ending the man's life. "Now he can go be with his friend," Stone said laying on his back looking up at the ceiling.

Tasha quickly ran to her man's aide. "Why do you always have to do things the hard way?" she said with a smile. Tasha was happy that her man had survived but, just wished he would have just zip tied the man's hands behind his back and avoided the fight.

"Don't ever ask me to go on vacation, ever again," Anthony Stone flashed a smile. Tasha couldn't help but laugh. She was happy that this nightmare was finally over. "I'm picking our next vacation!"

Tasha helped Stone sit up. "I love you to death!"

"I love you too, baby," Stone replied. "I would kiss you but, my mouth is still a little bloody." The two shared a nice laugh as they stuck by each other's side until the ship finally came to a stop.

CHAPTER 32

Captain Fisher stood with a smile on his face as he watched the paramedics escort Anthony Stone and the rest of the hostages off the ship. Captain Fisher was happy to see Anthony Stone alive and in one piece. "Glad to have you back on land," Captain Fisher said with a smile.

"It's nice to see you too Captain," Stone smiled.

"You did a great job," Captain Fisher said in a serious tone. "You are a wonderful detective and I'm going to push for you to get a promotion; you deserve it."

"Thanks Captain. I appreciate it," Anthony Stone smiled.

"We're you able to locate The Genius while you were on that ship?"

Stone shook his head. "Not that I know of," he paused for a second. "Not to mention I have no idea what he even looks like."

"Well the only thing that matters right now is that you're safe and you rescued as many hostages as you could," Captain Fisher extended his hand. "You're a hero in my book!"

"You're a hero in my book too," Tasha kissed Anthony Stone on his cheek as Captain Fisher walked off. "I'm proud of you!"

"For what? I did what anyone else would have done in my situation," Anthony Stone shrugged.

"You don't give yourself enough credit baby," Tasha rubbed his lower back as several hostages walked up to Anthony Stone and thanked him for saving their lives and all the hard work he had put in while on the ship.

"I see I'm not the only one that thinks you're a hero," Tasha smiled.

"The sad part is, now after all this, I need another vacation," he said as the two enjoyed a strong laugh. Stone limped over towards his ride home when he heard someone call out his name from behind. He spun around and saw Brett standing there. Immediately a smile came to Stone's face.

"Hey man, I just wanted to say thank you for everything you did back there on that ship," Brett said. "You're one brave man and I appreciate you," he said extending his hand.

"I thank you for taking care of my girl for me while I wasn't around. I don't know where she'd be if it wasn't for you," Stone said as the two men shook hands. Just as Stone was about to walk away he looked down and noticed a spider tattoo on Brett's wrist.

"Make sure you get home safe."

"You do the same," Anthony Stone turned and walked back over towards Tasha.

"What's wrong?" Tasha asked. Immediately she could sense that something wasn't right.

"He's The Genius," Anthony Stone said in a harsh whisper making sure not to look over his shoulder.

"Who Brett?!" Tasha asked with a confused look on her face. "Are you sure? He seemed like such a nice guy," Tasha said not wanting to believe her ears.

"I'm positive, that's him." Anthony Stone walked over to his car and popped the trunk. Inside the trunk he grabbed a 9mm and stuck it in the small of his back. "Hey, take the car and go home. I'll meet you there later."

Tasha grabbed Stone and hugged him tightly. "Please be careful! I love you," she whispered in his ear.

"I love you too, baby."

CHAPTER 33

Captain Fisher stood talking to a reporter giving a detailed interview when Anthony Stone walked up and tapped him on the shoulder. "I'll be with you in a second Detective Stone."

"I've spotted The Genius," Anthony Stone whispered. That one line grabbed the Captain's attention.

"Excuse me for a second," he smiled then walked away from the reporter. "Where is he?"

Anthony Stone nodded in Brett's direction. "The one in the suit."

"Are you sure that's him?" Captain Fisher asked with a raised brow. "Did you check for the tattoo on his wrist?"

Anthony Stone nodded, "that's him."

"You want to take him down, now?" Captain Fisher asked.

"No, let's follow him and see where he leads us," Stone suggested never taking his eye off the target. What bothered Stone the most was how The Genius was able to blend in so well and appear normal to the average eye. Even he would have been fooled if he didn't have inside information about The Genius' wrist tattoo.

"I want to nail this asshole right now," Captain Fisher said through clenched teeth. He couldn't believe he was finally looking at the man who called himself The Genius and was close enough to reach out and grab him.

"Patience," Anthony Stone smiled. "Right now we have the upper hand so let's use it to our advantage."

"I sure as hell hope you know what you're doing!" Captain Fisher growled as his hands dangled down by his side close to his service pistol just in case he needed to use it.

CHAPTER 34

The Genius shook a few hands then walked over to the Range Rover that sat in the cut awaiting his arrival. He slid in the back seat and immediately the Range Rover pulled off. The driver of the Range Rover was none other than one of the female hostages who was trapped on the ship playing a decoy. "That was a piece of cake just like you said it would be," the blonde hair driver laughed.

"Michelle, when have I ever led you in the wrong direction?" The Genius flashed a million-dollar smile. He and Michelle had been an item for the past seven years.

"You are a genius baby," Michelle stroked his already large ego. "Those idiots don't even realize what we just did. We just got away with over ten million dollars."

The Genius smiled, "You ready to go to Hawaii?"

"Of course! You promised me a house on the beach," Michelle reminded him.

"Baby, after today, you can have anything you want," The Genius told her. "I just feel a little bad about Rambo." Over the years The Genius and Rambo had built a strong relationship and the fact that Rambo was now gone didn't sit too well with him.

"Baby, you did what you had to do," Michelle said in a comforting tone. "If it were reversed, Rambo would have done the same thing."

"I know," The Genius said quickly. "While on the ship I came up with our next job."

"What is it?" Michelle asked anxiously. She could already picture all the money the next job would bring in.

"We'll discuss it over dinner baby," The Genius said as he placed the MacBook on his lap and fired it up. After checking to make sure all his funds had been transferred and were safe, he smiled. It had taken him six months to come up with this master plan only for Detective Anthony Stone to come so close to throwing a monkey wrench in the entire plan. "Did you see that superman detective?" The Genius laughed.

Michelle shook her head. "He almost messed the whole plan up," she pointed out. "I was hoping you killed him."

"He actually saved my life a few times," The Genius said as him and Michelle shared a good laugh. "If I ever cross paths with that asshole again, I'll put a bullet right between his eyes."

The Range Rover pulled up in front of a five-star hotel. The Genius stepped out the backseat and handed the valet attendant a hundred-dollar bill as him and Michelle disappeared inside the hotel.

The couple boarded the elevator and as soon as the doors closed, they were all over each other. The Genius slammed Michelle's back up against the wall in the elevator and kissed her like he had just been released from prison after doing a ten-year bid. "I love you," he growled in between kisses. Michelle grabbed The Genius' hand and placed it under her skirt. Just as they were about to get into it, the elevator door opened with a loud ding. The Genius looked over his shoulder and saw an old couple staring at them.

"Excuse me," The Genius said politely as he and Michelle exited the elevator and headed down the hall towards their room.

The Genius stepped foot in the suite, stripped down to his birthday suit, then walked over to the kitchen area to grab a bite to eat while Michelle went to the bathroom. Seconds later, the sound of running water could be heard. The Genius bit down into his sandwich and closed his eyes for a second so he could enjoy the taste of it. When he spun around, he saw Michelle standing in the doorway of the bathroom holding a gun with a silencer attached to the barrel in her hand.

"What the hell are you doing?" The Genius asked with a confused look on his face.

"I love you but, I don't trust you," Michelle said honestly as she raised her arms aiming the gun at The Genius' chest.

"What do you mean?" The Genius asked while grabbing a napkin and wiping the corner of his mouth. "We've been together for seven years and I've been nothing but, good to you."

"I don't even know your real name," Michelle pointed out.

"The less you know, the better off you are," The Genius said in a calm tone. "I was protecting you."

"Bullshit!" Michelle snapped. "The only person you care about is yourself."

"Baby, we won the game and now it's time for us to run off into the sunset," he said. "Put that gun down and let's start all over."

"Fuck you!" Michelle spat. "As soon as I turn my back, you'll do me just like you did Rambo!"

"Listen baby, I did what I had to do."

"Now I'm about to do what I have to do," Michelle countered. She held the gun with two hands and pulled the trigger.

CLICK! CLICK! CLICK!

Michelle looked down at the gun in her hand with a confused look on her face.

"I removed the bullets when we were on the elevator," The Genius said in a calm tone as he grabbed a sharp knife from off the knife rack. "I had a funny feeling about you but, I couldn't quite place my finger on it until now."

"Baby, I'm sorry," Michelle dropped down to her knees, clamping her hands together as if she was about to pray.

"Baby?!" The Genius repeated with a smirk on his face. "That's funny! Was I your baby a few second ago?"

"I'm sorry..."

"No, I'm sorry," The Genius said as he slowly began to make his way towards Michelle. "And to think, I was actually going to buy you a house in Hawaii and give you the world."

"Baby let's leave the country and start over fresh," Michelle begged. "I always loved you."

The more Michelle talked, the angrier The Genius became. The fact that a woman that he had love for would try to cross him really bothered him. The Genius walked up to Michelle and without warning, plunged the knife in and out of her neck repeatedly. "Stupid ass cunt! Thought you was going to kill me! Took my kindness for weakness! Thought you were going to escape with all my money!" He growled until his arm finally got tired from stabbing the woman he had love for. The Genius looked down at what was left of Michelle and smiled. He got the name The Genius because he planned for any and every situation. He was truly a "Genius!"

The Genius stepped in the shower and stood directly under the showerhead letting the water massage his face. After what just happened, he now had a lot to think about and some re-planning to do. The Genius stepped out the shower, dried off, and proceeded to pack all of his things. It was times like this when he was glad that he didn't tell Michelle his real name. It wasn't no telling who she may have given it to. He called downstairs to the front desk to have the valet get his Range Rover, then exited his room. The Genius stepped out the room dressed in a navy blue custom made Italian suit with a briefcase in his hand.

CHAPTER 35

The Genius stepped off the elevator feeling like a new man. His only mission right now was to make it to the airport, leave the country, and start over fresh. He needed to go somewhere, where he would have no distractions. The Genius strolled through the lobby without a care in the world until he spotted Detective Anthony Stone and another man that had cop written all over him heading straight towards him.

The Genius smiled, "Gentlemen how can I help you?"

"Hey Brett," Anthony Stone said with a straight face. "Going somewhere?" His eyes looked down at the briefcase in The Genius' hand.

"Actually I am," The Genius replied. "Again is there something I can help you with?"

"Yes, why don't you start by giving all the hostages that were on that ship you high jacked their money back?" Stone countered letting it be known that they knew exactly who he was.

"I'm sorry but, I don't follow," The Genius said remaining cool. "Should I contact my attorney?"

"Cut the shit!" Anthony Stone barked removing his 9mm from his holster. "Now we can do this the easy way or we can do this the hard way."

"You don't look like no genius from where I'm standing," Captain Fisher said speaking for the first time. In his hands he held a pair of handcuffs.

"That was real clever of you to try and blend in as one of the hostages but, I guess you're not as smart as you thought," Anthony Stone said. "Lay face down on the floor! NOW!"

The Genius smiled as he tossed the briefcase at Anthony Stone's face then took off in a sprint in the opposite direction. Being as though The Genius had dress shoes on, he wasn't able to run at his highest speed. He pushed innocent bystanders out of his way as he ran as fast as he could through the crowded hotel looking for the nearest exit.

Anthony Stone picked up speed and dived on The Genius' back sending the both of them crashing through the glass window of the small gift shop at the end of the hallway. The Genius scrambled back to his feet when he felt Stone's arms slip around his neck placing him in a deadly choke hold. The Genius felt his oxygen being cut off and immediately tapped out but, Anthony Stone refused to release his grip.

Captain Fisher ran up to the gift shop breathing heavily. "STONE!" he yelled. "LET HIM GO! THIS ASSHOLE ISN'T WORTH IT!"

Stone ignored his boss and continued to apply pressure. He wanted this to be over with once and for all and the only way that was going to happen was if The Genius was dead.

"Think about your family detective!" Captain Fisher placed a friendly hand on Stone's shoulder. "Let him rot in jail! This scumbag isn't worth it."

Three seconds later Anthony Stone finally released his grip from around The Genius' neck. Captain Fisher quickly cuffed The Genius' hands behind his back and called in for back up. "You did the right thing, son." He pulled Anthony Stone in for a hug.

"I need some time off Captain," Stone said out of breath. He needed to spend some much needed quality time with Tasha and start to enjoy his life. "I'll call you in about a month, Captain."

"What about this piece of shit? Don't you want to bring him in?" Captain Fisher asked. Anthony Stone waved him off and continued to walk outside where he caught a cab and headed home where he belonged. While in the back of the cab, Stone thought long and hard about if he wanted to return back to his job or should he just start over fresh in an entirely new profession… He stared out the window when he heard his phone ring. "Hey baby," he answered.

"I'm watching the news and I see you caught The Genius!" Tasha said in an excited tone. "I'm so proud of you baby!"

"Thank you baby; just doing my job."

"Well, you need to get home so I can do my job," she said in a sexy tone. "I miss you."

"I'm on my way home now, baby," Anthony Stone said with his eyes closed in the backseat.

"Can you do me a favor before you come home please?" Tasha asked.

"No, I'm not getting you no Chipotle!" Anthony Stone said as him and Tasha enjoyed a much needed laugh.

THE END

BOOKS BY GOOD2GO AUTHORS

GOOD 2 GO FILMS PRESENTS

**THE HAND I WAS DEALT- FREE WEB SERIES
NOW AVAILABLE ON YOUTUBE!
YOUTUBE.COM/SILKWHITE212**

SEASON TWO NOW AVAILABLE

To order books, please fill out the order form below:

To order films please go to **www.good2gofilms.com**

Name:_____

Address:_____

City: _____ State: _____ Zip Code: _____

Phone:_____

Email:_____

Method of Payment: Check   VISA   MASTERCARD

Credit Card#:_____

Name as it appears on card: _____

Signature: _____

Item Name	Price	Qty	Amount
48 Hours to Die – Silk White	$14.99		
Business Is Business – Silk White	$14.99		
Business Is Business 2 – Silk White	$14.99		
Business Is Business 3 – Silk White	$14.99		
Childhood Sweethearts – Jacob Spears	$14.99		
Childhood Sweethearts 2 – Jacob Spears	$14.99		
Childhood Sweethearts 3 - Jacob Spears	$14.99		
Flipping Numbers – Ernest Morris	$14.99		
Flipping Numbers 2 – Ernest Morris	$14.99		
He Loves Me, He Loves You Not - Mychea	$14.99		
He Loves Me, He Loves You Not 2 - Mychea	$14.99		
He Loves Me, He Loves You Not 3 - Mychea	$14.99		
He Loves Me, He Loves You Not 4 – Mychea	$14.99		
He Loves Me, He Loves You Not 5 – Mychea	$14.99		
Lost and Turned Out – Ernest Morris	$14.99		
Married To Da Streets – Silk White	$14.99		
M.E.R.C. - Make Every Rep Count Health and Fitness	$14.99		
My Besties – Asia Hill	$14.99		
My Besties 2 – Asia Hill	$14.99		
My Besties 3 – Asia Hill	$14.99		
My Besties 4 – Asia Hill	$14.99		
My Boyfriend's Wife - Mychea	$14.99		
My Boyfriend's Wife 2 – Mychea	$14.99		
Never Be The Same – Silk White	$14.99		
Stranded – Silk White	$14.99		
Slumped – Jason Brent	$14.99		
Tears of a Hustler - Silk White	$14.99		
Tears of a Hustler 2 - Silk White	$14.99		

Tears of a Hustler 3 - Silk White	$14.99		
Tears of a Hustler 4- Silk White	$14.99		
Tears of a Hustler 5 – Silk White	$14.99		
Tears of a Hustler 6 – Silk White	$14.99		
The Panty Ripper - Reality Way	$14.99		
The Panty Ripper 3 – Reality Way	$14.99		
The Teflon Queen – Silk White	$14.99		
The Teflon Queen 2 – Silk White	$14.99		
The Teflon Queen 3 – Silk White	$14.99		
The Teflon Queen 4 – Silk White	$14.99		
The Teflon Queen 5 – Silk White	$14.99		
The Teflon Queen 6 - Silk White	$14.99		
The Vacation – Silk White	$14.99		
Tied To A Boss - J.L. Rose	$14.99		
Tied To A Boss 2 - J.L. Rose	$14.99		
Time Is Money - Silk White	$14.99		
Young Goonz – Reality Way	$14.99		
Subtotal:			
Tax:			
Shipping (Free) U.S. Media Mail:			
Total:			

Make Checks Payable To:
Good2Go Publishing
7311 W Glass Lane,
Laveen, AZ 85339